Fairy Tale Flirts! 5 Romantic Short Stories

Lisa Scott

ISBN:1481289993
ISBN-13: 978-1481289993

CONTENTS

1 "Cindi"   3

2 "Red"   Pg #48

3 "Belle"   Pg #85

4 "Snow"   Pg #122

5 "Goldie"   Pg #161

6 "About the Author"   Pg #202

"Cindi"
by Lisa Scott

Cindi Midas could still smell bleach and latex on her
hands as she rode the elevator to her apartment. Coming
home to posh Grimm Towers from her early morning
cleaning job at the Castle Hotel was always embarrassing.
Most people probably assumed she was the hired help as
she rode the ornate elevator to the 55th floor where she
lived with her stepmother. But since she didn't pay Cindi
for cleaning their apartment, technically, she wasn't the
hired help; she was the free-room-and-board help.
Luckily, Cindi was a horrible cook or her stepmother
would probably have her doing that, too.

It was just before noon and she let herself in the
door, desperate for a shower and a change of clothes.
Once she got her party planning business off the ground,
she'd burn her pale pink polyester uniform and move out.
She kicked off her shoes and wandered into the kitchen.

Her stepmother and stepsister sat at the table, the
chandelier twinkling overhead. "Sorry, Cindi. You
missed breakfast," her stepsister, Gloria, said, shoving a
croissant in her mouth.

"I ate when I got up at four this morning." She
opened the fridge and grabbed a yogurt. "This is lunch."

Her stepmother, Hildy, splayed three golden tickets
in her hand at the table. "Forget food, look what Mother
got! I've been waiting until you got home, Cindi."

Cindi dropped her spoon. "Impossible," she
whispered, while Gloria clapped and rushed over to hug
her mother.

2

Once the shock wore off, Cindi practically squealed. "I can't believe we're going to the Jiminy Shoe trunk sale today!" *Maybe wishes really do come true*, she thought, fully aware it was a shallow-as-a-puddle wish, but damn it, she was meant to live in designer wear. Her christening gown had been couture from the looks of the pictures in her old photo album. But that was then. Long before Hildy wriggled her way into her father's life.

However, Cindi could find some forgiveness in her heart with one of those tickets. The Jiminy Shoe trunk sale was the most exclusive sale in New Royalton and she'd never been to it. Sure, she'd dreamed of going, making lists in her head of all the shoes she'd buy if she won the lottery; or if her father had set up a trust fund for her instead of leaving it all to her stepmother.

Oh, she had real, responsible dreams, too: a successful party planning business, moving out, and finding love someday. But her shallow, greedy dreams glittered with the latest shoes and clothes and cosmetics. A pair of Jiminy Shoes was at the top of her list. Every self-respecting twenty-something-fashionista-wanna-be deserved a pair. And for a moment, while wearing those shoes, maybe she could imagine the life she would have led if her parents hadn't died. Surely, they would have bought her Jiminies.

Gloria had given her a hand-me-down pair that didn't fit her. Cindi kept them on a shelf in her bedroom because she enjoyed looking at them, and occasionally stroking the luscious, buttery leather. Finally, she'd have a pair of her own. Luckily, she had a few hundred dollars saved. She practically purred like a cat licking its chops before devouring a plate of tuna.

Her stepmother blinked at her. "Oh, no. I'm sorry,

3

Cindi. You misunderstood. I'm not bringing you."

Her stomach tumbled. "But you waited to tell me. And you have three tickets." She held up three fingers to make it clear.

Hildy blinked and smiled. "Yes, I wanted to share the news with you. But I had to beg for these tickets so I could take my daughters."

Knowing she didn't count as one of the daughters, Cindi fought back the tears. "Veronica's going? I thought you disowned her."

Her stepmother scrunched up her carefully sculpted nose that had taken four trips to the plastic surgeon to perfect. "Oh, that was just my temper talking when she refused to follow my plans for her future. She'll see the light soon enough, but she's not going today." Hildy shrugged. "I merely told the organizers it was for her, but I'm giving it to Kate Robinson." She snarled as she said her name.

"The lady down the hall? You don't even like her. You tried to kill her dog."

"That was an accident and no one can prove otherwise," her stepmother said in a sing-song-I'm-lying-voice.

It was humiliating, but Cindi made a pathetic pleading gesture with her hands. "Please? You know how much I love Jiminies. I'm sure you could help me find the perfect pair. I could never be as skinny and pretty as you, but maybe I could have shoes as nice as yours." After her father had died, any niceties her stepmother had shown Cindi had disappeared. But she'd learned that sometimes begging worked, just so long as loads of flattery—no matter how farfetched—was involved.

Her stepmother put her hands on her hips; Cindi

recognized her lecture mode when she saw it. "Mrs. Robinson thinks I owe her a thousand dollars to cover the vet bills for stepping on that walking wig she calls a dog." She sighed dramatically. "Since these are priceless tickets, we should be even now. Really, that woman." She shrugged. "Sorry, you'll have to get your own ticket."

"But there are only two hundred! And you have to know someone to get in." She hadn't whined like this since she was ten and wanted a pony. And she'd gotten one. They'd kept it stabled just outside the city. It was the first thing her stepmother had gotten rid of after Father died.

Hildy grinned like she was downing a glass of bad lemonade. "True. And you don't know anyone, do you? Besides, I don't trust that you could compose yourself at an event like that. You'd probably embarrass me. You'll have a nice quiet day at home. Perhaps you can organize Gloria's closet like you promised."

That had been a joke, although Gloria's closet did look like the aftermath of a home invasion. But some cleaners didn't do bathrooms, others didn't do closets. Cindi fell in the latter group. She rested her chin in her hand, feeling like a chastised child left sulking at the table.

Her stepsister gloated. "We'll be back later. In fabulous new shoes!"

They left the apartment in a swirl of perfume and giggles. Cindi walked into the living room and slumped on the couch. She looked down at her bare feet, her toenails painted with a French manicure she'd done herself. Nope, no spa visits for her either. She blinked back the final tears she was going to let fall over this. Not everyone is destined for fabulous footwear. *But someday, I'll have great shoes.*

5

After allowing herself to pout for a few more minutes, she jumped in the shower, changed, then pulled out her laptop and looked for potential party clients. While her stepmother insisted her daughters look for rich husbands instead of work—something Veronica had ignored at first—her stepmother didn't expect Cindi to land a wealthy man. "I know you'll have to support yourself," she'd told her.

But Cindi wanted to work. Relying on Daddy to cater to her every whim had worked for twelve years. She'd been spoiled and that had taken a long time to get over once he was gone. She'd never be dependent on a man again. Didn't matter if she married a millionaire, she had hopes and dreams and visions for the future. She just wasn't entirely certain what they were.

Hopefully, party planning was her calling. She'd always envisioned herself attending fancy charity balls and events. At age twenty-four, she'd already tried waitressing and retail along with the cleaning job. None of them had been the right fit.

She started compiling her daily list of ten businesses to contact about her party planning services. Clearly, she was very skilled at making lists, but no one hired you to do that. She'd been making ten new contacts a day, and had landed half a dozen event-planning jobs that way. But it still wasn't enough money for her to move out of Grimm Towers.

The doorbell rang and she set down her computer, ran to the door and peeked through the peephole. It was Mrs. Robinson from down the hall. She opened the door. "Hi Mrs. Robinson what can I do for you?" Her fluffy little brown dog sat at her feet. What was it, a Poo-hau-hau? A Shitz-aranian? Maybe she could be a designer dog breeder if the party planning didn't work out.

Mrs. Robinson held up a golden ticket. "Your stepmother left this with a note under my door. She thinks a ticket to the Jiminy Shoes trunk sale is suitable payment for Cricket's vet bills. Totally unacceptable. I expect her to pay me. This ticket is the last thing I need. Give it back and tell *her* to use it instead." She handed it to Cindi.

"She's already at the show."

Mrs. Robinson raised an eyebrow. "Don't you want to go?"

"More than anything, but I wasn't invited."

She frowned. "I tell you what. I'm going to act like I never saw that ticket. I'll tell her Cricket must've eaten it, if she was foolish enough to leave it under my door. You take it and go to the sale. But do not let your stepmother know I gave it to you."

Cindi took the woman's head in her hands and kissed her cheek. "You are a fairy godmother. Thank you, thank you, thank you!" There were a few benefits of living in the swankiest apartment building in the city; the castoffs from Grimm Tower's residents were splendid.

She took the ticket from Mrs. Robinson with a trembling hand.

She winked at Cindi. "Now go spiff yourself up and have a good time. Maybe you'll find the shoes of your dreams!"

***

Cindi changed into her favorite Dior knock-off dress, grabbed her cash and stuffed it into her fake Gucci. Then she looped her phony Prada shopping tote on her arm, slid on dark sunglasses, and tucked her hair under a floppy beret. She could not let her stepmother see her.

Butterflies did the Mambo in her stomach as she took the cab to the hotel downtown where the trunk sale was being held.

She caught her breath as she handed over her ticket at the door, and walked into the first room of the sale. Sliding off her sunglasses, she gazed around, taking it all in. The sight of so many gorgeous shoes almost made her dizzy. She took a deep breath. Now the challenge was finding a pair that fit. Most designers only had so many size fives in stock. Her tiny feet seriously tormented her sense of fashion.

Turning in circles, she didn't know where to start. What should she buy—a pair of practical pumps? Party shoes? Boots? Her heart raced with the possibilities. Then her eyes were drawn to the most beautiful shoes she'd ever seen. A pair of sparkly crystal pumps sat atop a display in the center of the room. She walked up beside the display and sighed. Now those were the shoes of her dreams.

But what were they doing up so high where no one could reach them? Under a plexi-glass box? Standing on her tiptoes and then jumping, she knocked the box off and snatched them from their perch. She sat down on a bench to try them on. Wishful thinking, of course. What were the chances they'd fit? But still, she wanted to hold them and touch them and pretend for a moment she was getting ready for a magnificent charity ball that she'd planned, where she'd dance the night away in these shoes.

She looked for a price tag on them, but couldn't find one. She set them on the floor and slid her foot inside. A perfect fit! Putting on the other shoe, she sashayed back and forth in front of the bench. *Please be in my price range, please be in my price range.*

A large, unhappy man in a dark suit approached her. She smiled at him. "Excuse me, can you find out how much these shoes are?"

"Ma'am, please take off the display shoes." He was quite gruff for a salesperson.

"But I'd like to buy these. Maybe I could get a discount since they're display shoes? I don't care how many people have worn them." She'd gotten a saleswoman to knock thirty-percent off a winter coat on display. Maybe it would work here, too. But truly, they were in pristine condition.

The big man was not amused. "Didn't you see the sign? These are one-of-a-kind shoes for display only." He pointed to the front of the display table. Walking around to the front, she saw the sign explaining the shoes were not for sale.

She knew she was blushing. "I'm so sorry, I didn't see that. I've never been to a trunk sale before. I ... I ..." she stammered, too embarrassed and disappointed to find the right words.

"Take them off. Now."

Mortified, she went back to the bench, memorizing how her feet looked in those shoes, when another man approached her. He crossed his arms. "I never imagined those would fit anyone. They look great on you."

She smiled up at him and sucked in a breath. He was gorgeous. "Thanks," she said in a voice sultrier than she'd intended.

"Enjoy them for a few more minutes."

The big man stepped closer. "Boss, I'm not supposed to let anyone touch those. I stepped away for a minute because there was a tussle at the cash register and

I come back to find this woman trying to take off with the shoes."

"What? Wait, no. I just wanted to try them on," Cindi protested. "I wasn't taking them."

"Why weren't they locked up?" the tall blond asked.

The big man looked down, turning red. "My mother stopped by and wanted to see them. I guess I forgot to lock them back up."

The other man jerked his thumb toward the room next door. "Bruno, go make sure no one's fighting over the boots in the ballroom."

The big man shook his head and walked away.

He sat down next to her. *Mmm. He smells good, too.*

"So, you're a size five." He whistled softly. "Don't see that very often."

"And you don't see too many shoes in size five. I was surprised they fit." She looked down at her feet and grinned.

"They're made from fused crystals and diamonds, with an invisible mesh inside to keep them flexible. They took weeks to create. We made such a small size to save money. Even so, they cost two-hundred thousand dollars."

She gulped, and picked her feet up off the floor as if to protect the little masterpieces. "You work for Jiminy Shoes?" A man who could keep her in shoes? *Swoon....*

"Yes, I'm Henry Hubbard. Head of marketing."

Oh, he's handsome and he knows shoes. She stuck out her foot and twirled it around. "These are gorgeous."

"They certainly are. But of course, they're not for sale." His voice was deep and soothing.

She could only nod. How could she feel

breathless just sitting next to him? Unless it was the shoes causing that reaction. "I couldn't even afford the heel on one of them. But I've never seen anything so gorgeous."

"I know," he said, staring at her.

Her gaze locked on his in a perfect, blissful moment. Until a scuffle across the room caught their attention.

He held up a finger. "Wait here just a moment. They're probably arguing over the last peep-toe slingbacks. I swear this trunk show makes Black Friday look like the little leagues. I'll be right back."

Cindi took one last look at her feet encased in true shoe love and sighed. Then she slipped them off and set them on the bench next to her. "Bye, bye my sweets," she whispered. She looked up to see if Henry had the situation under control.

Then she gasped. Her stepmother was gripping one end of a shoebox, tugging it from the hands of a pregnant woman. Gloria stood with her arms crossed, inspecting her nails.

"Damn," Cindi whispered. She couldn't let them see her here. Grabbing her purse off the bench next to the shoes, she snatched the shopping tote from the floor, stumbled, then ran. She wasn't sure if she was more upset to leave without a pair of Jiminies, or to leave without seeing Henry again. For pure eye candy purposes only, of course. Henry, that is—not the shoes. She could have made a life long commitment to those shoes. If she could've taken a mortgage out on those shoes she would have.

She headed for the door and nearly bumped into Veronica with a gaggle of kids in tow. She counted them.

Seven children? She hid behind a huge potted palm tree as she tried to make her escape. Palm trees aren't nearly as big as they lead you to believe in the movies. She crouched down further, then froze when her stepmother marched in her direction, red-faced and shoebox-less. Cindi was thrilled she hadn't won the battle.

Luckily, she didn't see Cindi and veered towards Veronica, instead. "What, is my daughter working for a preschool now?"

Veronica rolled her eyes. "Hello, Mother. It's been a while. No, this isn't my job. I've found a perfectly wonderful rich man who happens to have seven children. He thinks we're at the park."

The two older children removed the harness from around their waist. "She's bribing us to keep it a secret," one of the girls said.

"Stop it, you two!" Veronica barked, tying the kids up again.

Hildy sighed. "Veronica. How many times have I told you that you don't watch a man's children? You get a nanny. Or you ignore them, like I did with Cindi."

"Mother, don't worry. I won't be watching them for long. I'll find a nanny."

She patted Veronica's cheek. "Good girl. Looks like you've finally come around to my way of thinking. Come on. Let me buy you a pair of shoes. Something you could wear at your wedding, perhaps? Maybe the third time will be the charm. I can't believe that last one died and left you penniless."

"Oh, we're not that close yet, mother. His wife recently died. These things take time, you know." Veronica tightened her grip on the harness that linked the kids like reindeer on a sleigh, the poor things.

Clearly, the wicked stepmother gene runs in the family, thought Cindi, gripping the edge of the concrete planter.

"Well, soon enough you will be! You're my daughter after all. We Midas girls know how to land a man. Unlike Cindi, who will probably be my burden for the rest of my life...." Her stepmother sighed dramatically as if she'd just remembered the burden she bore caring for her.

Cindi's gut twisted. What a horrible day. She had to move out of that apartment. She had to strike out on her own. Maybe it was a good thing she hadn't bought a pair of Jiminies. She could use that five hundred dollars towards a deposit on an apartment. Still, as she fled the hotel after her stepmother and Veronica walked away, her heart ached for shoes loved and lost.

***

By the time Henry refereed the fight over the patent mules—by pointing out that the shoes were half a size too small for the older woman trying to wrestle them away—he realized the beautiful blonde with the tiny feet was gone. He returned to the bench where she'd been sitting, and picked up one crystal shoe. Walking around the bench, he peered under it, but couldn't find its mate. With one shoe in his hand, his eyes swept the room, searching for the girl.

Bruno ran up to him. "I just spotted your friend running out the door with one of the shoes sticking out of her bag. She was in a real hurry. She hopped in a cab before I could stop the little thief."

Henry frowned. "Why would she take just one?"

"Even one is worth a hundred grand."

"Right, but if you're going to steal them, you'd take both.

13

"She's a thief. Who knows how they think."

Henry shook his head. "She's not the type."

Bruno poked a stubby finger in Henry's chest. "You say that only because she's *your* type."

He ignored Bruno even though it was true. "She's a size five. She won't be hard to find. I'll go look through our preferred customer list and sort out all the size fives."

But half an hour later, he learned none of their preferred customers who'd been invited to the sale wore a size five.

"How can we find her, boss?" Bruno asked him. "Want me to make some calls?"

Henry shook his head. "On the off chance she did steal it, we don't want to give her a heads up. A one-of-a-kind diamond Jiminy isn't something you can unload quickly. I'm sure she still has it." He rubbed his chin. "We're going to have to go find her."

Bruno threw up his hands. "How?"

"Grab the address list for the customers who received tickets to the trunk sale. We'll have to conduct a door-to-door search—disguised as a contest."

"Do we go to the press with this?"

Henry sighed. "Yes. Maybe she'll see the report and turn herself in, or double-check her bags. It might have just fallen in."

Bruno gave him a look.

"What? It might have. I'm hoping for a happy ending here." And not just for the company, either.

"I'm sure you are."

"I'll handle this. Watch me spin PR gold, my friend."

***

Henry called a press conference, and all the news

14

outlets showed up. A missing hundred-thousand-dollar shoe? That's great water cooler stuff.

He held up the shoe and explained how it had been made out of crystals and tiny diamonds, how it was an unusual size—and incredibly expensive.

"Was the shoe stolen?" called out a reporter.

Henry shook his head. "We think the person would have grabbed both if it was a theft. There was a woman at the sale who fit into these shoes perfectly. We believe she took it inadvertently. When we find her, we have a special gift to apologize for all this trouble." What that gift was remained to be determined, but cops caught criminals all the time by offering free concert tickets or merchandise to people wanted on warrants. They showed up thinking they were going to get a free Blu-Ray only to get a free ride to jail.

Not that this woman was a criminal. But a little incentive never hurt, did it? He'd had such an instant attraction to her; he pleaded with the universe to let this all be a big misunderstanding. Even at his most desperate moments as a child, when he and his mother and brother had nothing to eat, he wouldn't have considered stealing. Was Bruno right? Was he too blinded by her beauty to face the truth?

***

Cindi headed for her secret stash of chocolate when Gloria and her mom came home with bags of shoes and purses and other Jiminy Shoes goodies. Gloria paraded around the apartment, putting on a new pair every few hours.

Cindi locked herself in her room and searched for twenty new party contacts a day for the next few days when she wasn't busy scrubbing toilets and changing sheets at the hotel. Things just had to change; she couldn't go on like this.

Three days after the sale, the doorbell rang and she assumed it was another one of Gloria's friends who'd come to see her new shoes. She'd had more visitors over the past few days than if she'd been showing off a new baby.

But it wasn't high-pitched cackles of her friends that she heard; it was a man's voice. Cindi cracked open the door and did a double take—it was the gorgeous man from the sale. Henry Hubbard. What was he doing here?

She opened the door a bit more, leaning forward to hear. Fortunately, Gloria turned off her music when the man arrived, so Cindi could see and hear most of their conversation.

Gloria and her mother smiled like fools while the man explained the reason for his visit. "It seems we made a perfect match at the shoe sale. A mysterious woman fit into our beautiful diamond sample shoes. But she escaped before we could award a special prize—a modeling shoot with the shoes and a one-thousand dollar shopping spree at our store."

Cindi's heart was in her throat. He was looking for her! But if she burst out there and said, 'Oh, it was me, me, me!' her stepmother would find out about the ticket, and lord only knew what she'd do to Cindi and Mrs. Robinson and her dog.

"Of course! I remember you trying them on," her stepmother said, elbowing Gloria.

"No, I don't think so." Gloria blinked her beady eyes at her mother, confused.

"Remember?" Hildy hissed. "They were a perfect fit on you, Gloria."

Henry looked doubtful. "Then please, try this one and we'll see."

Even from far across the apartment, Cindi could see that Gloria's big toe barely fit in the shoe. Yet Gloria persisted, plastering on a smile, and trying to force her foot into the poor little shoe.

Finally, Henry pulled it away, probably out of concern she might break it. He frowned. "I don't think you're the one. I was really hoping to find that girl."

And that's when Cindi leaned a bit too hard against the door and tumbled out, tail over teakettle.

Three heads turned in her direction. When she stood up rubbing her sore head, Henry beamed. "It's you. Size five, am I right?" He was as handsome as she remembered, but she couldn't keep her eyes off that dazzling shoe.

She grinned. "I am."

"Come, try on the shoe."

Her stepmother crossed her arms and sneered. "Oh, it can't be her. She wasn't at the show. She didn't know anyone who could get her a ticket."

"Trust me, I wouldn't forget someone like her. Please, come see if it fits."

She didn't care what punishment her stepmother would come up with; she had to get that shoe back on her foot.

She sat on the couch and held out her foot. Henry smiled at her, and slid on the sparkly, clear shoe. "Perfect fit," he said, with his fingers circled gently around her ankle. She could imagine them sliding up her calf, over her knee and onto her thigh.

The big security guard from the sale stormed in the apartment. "I knew it! Now hand over the other shoe or you're under arrest."

Henry held out a hand to stop the man from getting any closer. "Bruno, we haven't even heard her side of the story."

"My stepdaughter's a thief? No surprise there."

Cindi's hand flew to her throat. "What are you talking about?"

Henry's shoulders slumped. "We're missing the mate to this pair. Bruno saw you running from the sale—with the shoe sticking out of your bag."

She could feel the blood draining from her face. She'd tossed the bag in her closet after getting home from the sale empty handed. "My bag's in my room. I haven't looked in it since I got home that day." Her heart raced as she headed to her room—followed by Gloria, her stepmother, Bruno, and Henry.

She pulled the bag out of her closet and sure enough, there was the shoe. She held it up and forced a smile. "Oops."

"It's a pretty big oops," Bruno said.

Henry stepped in front of Bruno. "No harm done. It's gotten us some good press coverage, actually." Henry held out his hand for the shoe.

Press coverage? That got Cindi's attention. *Think, think, think. There has to be a way to spin this to your advantage.* She couldn't lose these shoes, not again. She looked at Henry and smiled. "There's no reason for the good publicity to end. I have an idea." She led him back into the living room and slipped on both shoes. "People following this story must be dying to know where this shoe has been. They'll all tune in to hear about it. But now that's its been found, the story is over. People stop paying attention and the shoes go back on display."

"Under lock and key this time," Bruno mumbled.

She held up one finger in a just-a-minute gesture. "But what if I wore these shoes for a week, and you follow my adventures! These shoes were made for walking, and dancing, and shopping!" She actually clapped, she was so excited by the idea. "And maybe Jiminy Shoes could make a more affordable version that everyone would be clamoring to buy!" *And perhaps I'd get a free pair....*

Henry nodded, visibly impressed. "And maybe once you're done with the shoes, we could send them to someone else with size five feet somewhere else in the world, and see what a week's like in their shoes, so to speak." He smacked his hands together. "It's a killer idea."

Hildy stepped forward. "Who cares what Cindi does? She's as interesting as wet paint." She pushed Gloria toward Henry. "You should follow my daughter around."

Henry totally ignored Hildy, bless him. "Then when the week's up, the whole thing ends at a big party where you slip out of the shoes at midnight."

"Shoes in the City," Cindi offered, stepping closer to him.

"A Week In Her Shoes," Henry countered, setting his hands on her arms.

"Shoe Love," Cindi whispered, just inches from him.

They stood for a moment, as if poised for a kiss. Then Henry stepped back. "Let me call the boss on this. It's a great idea."

"Who is the boss?" Cindi asked innocently. It was one of the most closely guarded secrets in the fashion world.

19

Henry just gave her a look.

She shrugged. "It was worth a try."

Her stepmother pushed past her and poked Henry in the chest. "Now wait just one minute. I will not subject my family to this kind of publicity stunt." She shook her head. "Not while you're living in my house."

Cindi gritted her teeth, ready to spew venom, when Henry said, "She's a legal adult. We don't need your permission. And we can put her up at the Castle hotel for the week."

Hildy looked down her nose at her and let out a little laugh. "How perfectly funny. Cindi works at the castle hotel. As a maid."

Henry shrugged. "Not after this she won't be."

Gritting her teeth and stepmother lowered her voice. "Don't think you'll be coming back here after that."

Cindi's heart clenched. Being kicked out of her own father's apartment? The home where she grew up? She looked around the living room at the window seat where she'd sit and read for hours; at the balcony where she and Daddy would blow bubbles and watch them until they floated away, too far to be seen. She realized her father's best memories were in her heart, not in the walls her stepmother had redone in hideous shades of mauve and green. Putting her hands on her hips, she looked her stepmother in the eye. "It's about time I moved out on my own." Exactly how she was going to support herself was a mystery, but she'd figured it out. Now that she had this shot of confidence, it was time for a brand new start.

With brand new, killer shoes.

***

Henry hung up with the boss, thrilled that their idea

got the green light. Bruno helped Cindi load her things into their car, with a delivery van coming for the rest.

"I'm sorry this got you kicked out of your place," Henry told her.

She didn't look upset. "It's more like a much-needed kick in the pants to get out of a bad situation. See? The shoes are changing everything for me already."

"Wait, let me video tape you leaving your apartment in the new shoes!"

As Cindi stood outside her apartment door, she took her lovely little feet out of her old flats and slipped them into the beautiful crystal heels.

Henry swallowed a groan. Damn, she'd probably assume he had a foot fetish, the way he was grinning like an idiot. Truth was, he had a green-eyed-blonde fetish. And he was going to get to spend an entire week with the most beautiful one he'd ever seen—and get paid for it.

Henry followed her outside into the bright sunny day, the camera in his phone taping the entire time. Then he slid it in his pocket. They'd have to get her a tiny camera that hung from her waist and taped her feet. He'd record from other angles, too. He was no professional videographer, but his amateur work would likely give it more of a real feeling. The whole thing was an ingenious idea. Who was this woman? He couldn't wait to find out.

When he finished taping, she handed him the shoes. "See you later, darlings." She giggled.

It was going to be an interesting week. He smiled at her. "This is going to change your life. You ready?"

She turned to him with the most beautiful grin. "I've been waiting to change my life for a long time."

He'd been saying the same thing to himself for a

while, but how many people actually ever did it? His brother had left home to play trumpet in a band. He had groupies who followed him from town to town. But Henry was reluctant to leave their mother behind all alone so he could chase his own dreams—whatever they may. He didn't even know. Would he take advantage of this kind of opportunity like Cindi was? He wasn't sure. He admired her courage and spontaneity.

"First things first," he said. "We need to update the press that we've found the shoes, and then we'll hold a press conference tonight explaining that you'll be wearing these shoes for one week starting at midnight."

She closed her eyes and smiled, and he had to resist the urge to kiss her. "I can't believe this is happening," she whispered.

"Believe it," he told her. "And it's only going to get more interesting." He'd booked her a room at the hotel, where Bruno would deliver her things. "Rest up. The adventure begins tonight."

She nodded, but he noticed her hands shaking. He grabbed one and squeezed tighter than he meant to. "It's going to be fine. It's going to be fun! Start thinking about how you want to spend this week in those shoes."

"You'll be with me, right?" Her eyes were big and full of hope.

"Wouldn't miss it for the world."

***

He was right. The press was dying to know what had happened to that shoe. At nine o'clock that night, he introduced the world to Cindi—the girl in the crystal shoes—standing next to him in the hotel lobby. Her shoes sparkled in the light of the cameras as he explained what happened to the shoes, and the week ahead. "She's going to be a princess for a week and turn the shoes over at midnight next Saturday during a fabulous ball."

All the entertainment shows planned on following this lucky maid turned celeb and her shoes, and plenty of news programs wanted in on it, too. He'd be updating Jiminy's website several times a day with new photos and clips. He was almost as excited as she was. This was going to put him on the map as a marketing god.

Once the press conference broke up, Cindy exhaled. "Wow. That was crazy." She stifled a yawn. "I guess I'll head back to my room and we'll get started tomorrow?"

He shook his head. "This journey starts at midnight. The morning shows will want footage of the first night out. So what'll it be, dinner, dancing?"

She blew out a breath. "I guess we'll play it by ear."

"Great. You've got about an hour and a half to nap. Then we're hitting the town. I'll have a few outfits for you to choose from when you wake up."

"Really?"

He nodded. "Can't have you and these shoes out on the town dressed in anything but the best."

***

Cindi woke from the most spectacular dream. Then, looking around the hotel room, she realized it hadn't been a dream. She was out of her stepmother's apartment in a posh hotel with fabulous shoes and the adventure of a lifetime ahead of her.

She jumped out of bed and wandered into the sitting area of her hotel room. She'd cleaned this room before; now she was a guest. She pinched herself just in case this was a dream-in-a-dream. Luckily, it hurt. This was real. Three dresses hung from the back of the bathroom door with a note from Henry. "Pick the one you like best, but I've got my money on the pink cocktail dress. See you at midnight."

She tried on all three, but Henry was right. At five to twelve, she stood by the door waiting for this crazy plan to begin. She felt like she was waiting for a date. Only, Henry was really coming to pick up the shoes, not her.

His video camera was rolling when she opened the door. "Where will the adventure begin, princess? Come with me, your chariot awaits."

He led her to a Mercedes limousine. She hesitated before getting in. "This is incredible."

"Enjoy it. Remember, it all ends a week from now midnight, so make the most of it. Now where are we going first?"

***

She collapsed in bed at four in the morning. They'd gone dancing at several different nightclubs, and she ended the night walking along the river, recounting the evening's adventures for the camera. As she slid out of her dress, she realized her feet should be killing her. But they felt fine. These shoes truly were meant for her. She climbed into bed in her nightgown, still wearing the shoes.

In the morning, she woke to piles of gifts in the sitting room of her suite. Bottles of perfume and pricey makeup she'd only dreamed of owning were stacked on the coffee table. Bags and boxes covered most of the floor. It was better than a lifetime of birthday presents all waiting in one big pile in her hotel room. She knocked on Henry's door next to hers. "What's all that stuff in my room?" she asked when he opened the door.

"Swag, baby." He grinned, and her stomach flipped.

"And it's only just begun. The deliveries keep coming in. Designers everywhere are hoping you'll wear their clothes or jewelry and be photographed in it. It's super advertising for them.

"And I get to keep it all?"

He nodded. "And it's only day one." He pulled a key out of his pocket. "Oh, and a year-long lease from Cadillac." He tossed her the set of keys.

She was too stunned to speak. Everything she'd ever wanted was literally at her feet—and on her feet. All of the goodies she ogled in magazines and on TV. Well, everything except that pony of hers. If she weren't so shocked, she'd scream.

He handed her a sheet of paper. "Here are some possibilities for you today." It was an itinerary with potential locations to visit: museums, art galleries, trendy restaurants, and stores. Lots of stores.

They started off with breakfast down the street, Cindi's new discreet belt camera, smaller than a stopwatch, taping her feet as she walked. She ordered the most expensive breakfast she'd ever had, and Henry took a moment to tape her drinking a mimosa. "Cheers!" she said, raising it in the air.

Then he set his camera down. "That should be enough for a while."

"So, you're going to be with me the whole week?"

He set down his drink. "Is that a problem?"

"No, no. It just seems like a lot to ask of you. I mean, someone in your life's got to be upset about this. You relocated to the hotel for a week."

He forced a smile. "I haven't had a girlfriend in a while, if that's what you mean. I've got a lot of responsibilities. No time for that sort of thing. And this is going to launch me to a new level. Thanks so much for this fabulous idea and for being such a good sport."

She took another sip of her drink. "A good sport? You're paying to show me the time of my life this week— and you didn't give me a hard time about taking off with your shoe. Why didn't you think I stole it? Bruno did."

"I just had a feeling you were a good person."

She looked down at her half eaten crepes and smiled.

It was a bit surprising when Henry asked for a to-go bag for the leftover muffins and rolls. Maybe he had low blood sugar and needed a snack for later? Who knew? But later, she saw him slip the bag to a homeless man as they waited to cross the street.

Her throat was too tight for her to say anything, so she looked away, touched by the unexpected gesture. Henry was more than just a handsome, successful guy, and she couldn't wait to find out more. But first, the journey of the shoes beckoned.

They did some shopping after breakfast, and Cindi was stunned people knew who she was. Some even asked for her autograph and wanted to pose for pictures. She signed the backs of receipts and slips of paper as "The Girl In The Crystal Shoes."

"How do they know who I am?" she asked, after they left a jewelry store.

He grinned and held out his arm for her. "Not too many people are walking around New Royalton in crystal shoes being followed by a camera."

"True."

It was an exhausting day, but it flew by. When she finally got back to the hotel after dinner, she kicked off her shoes. "A little distance will make the heart grow fonder," she told Henry.

"Get your beauty sleep. I'll see you tomorrow," he told her.

***

Henry wasn't sure who was having more fun—him or Cindi. They strolled through museums together, stopping for another fabulous lunch the next day. Cindi was thoughtful, smart, and funny. She must have spotted him passing out leftover rolls to the homeless, because after breakfast, she did the same thing, without saying a word. He'd never been so touched by a woman's gesture. Most of his dates ignored his interactions with the homeless, or scolded him for it.

But then again, Cindi wasn't his date. Unfortunately.

During lunch, his phone rang, and he grimaced when he looked at the caller ID. He hated disappointing his mother but there was no way he could visit this week and let her find out about this over-the-top shoe promotion. "Hello, Mother."

"Henry, aren't you coming to see me?"

"Sorry, I can't right now. I'm totally wrapped up with work. Do you need anything? I could have something delivered for you. Whatever you need, just let me know."

"No, no. I'm fine. I look forward to our visits, is all. I get lonely, you know."

Did she give his brother this guilt trip? His brother probably didn't even call.

"Next week, Mother. We'll go out for lunch, it'll be great."

She sighed. "Alright then. Take care, Henry."

He hung up, his good mood disappearing, and tucked away his phone. "I try to visit my mother once a week. She lives outside the city, about an hour away. It's

27

impossible this week."

Cindi lifted a shoulder and smiled. "I wouldn't mind if we went to visit her."

He laughed. "I don't think people would enjoy watching you cavort about with my seventy-year-old mother. They're looking for something a little more exciting from you and the shoes."

"But I hate keeping you from your mom."

He drummed his fingers on the table and leaned forward, deciding she deserved an explanation. "My mother knows I work in marketing for a shoe company, but she doesn't know they're high-end designer shoes. I'd be too embarrassed to have her know I help peddle six hundred dollar shoes."

Cindi stirred her drink with the red cocktail straw. "I think she'd be proud you work for such a well known company. Why would she care how much the shoes cost?"

Sighing, he looked down. "We didn't have much money growing up. Six hundred dollars would have kept our cupboards filled for months. I think she'd feel bad, seeing the way I live now compared to how we grew up. I'm a bit embarrassed by some of the excess in my life." He had a posh apartment, a nice car, and while his cupboards were often bare, it was only because he usually ate out.

Cindi nodded and pointed her straw at him. "I see where you're coming from. If my father were still alive, he'd cringe at how I live now, scratching to get by. I grew up rich. When he died, my stepmother decided I wasn't worth spending money on. Of course, she and her daughters always have the best. That's why I've never had a pair of Jiminies."

He narrowed his eyes. "I knew I didn't like her. Thankfully, you're nothing like her."

She shrugged. "Well, we do both like nice shoes." And that was as far as the similarities went.

"My mother would say it was a complete waste if she knew how much Jiminies cost." He shook his head. "I think she'd be disappointed in me. I'm sure she wishes one of her sons went on to do something important, something that helps people. But neither of us did. My brother's in a band, traveling the world. I've never been out of this country."

"Why not?"

"I need to be close. I can't leave her alone."

"She told you that?"

He was shocked he was telling her so much, but Cindi really seemed like she cared. It was so easy to let all the hurts of the past tumble out. He shifted in his seat. "I'm protective of her. When we were poor and struggling to make ends meet, I felt so useless. There was nothing I could do to put food on the table." He realized his voice had gotten low and quiet.

"You were just a kid," she said, with tenderness in her voice.

He ran his thumb along the condensation on his glass. "But I was the oldest. I felt responsible. Sometimes, I'd bring home leftover treats from school if we'd had a party or something just to get some food in the house." He couldn't look up at her. The shame was still there. "I don't think there's anything I can do now to make it up to her. I just try to be there for her." Why did this woman make him feel so safe?

She reached her hand across the table to him and squeezed the tips of his fingers. "You never know, Henry.

Maybe after all these years she'd love a pair of fancy shoes. She deserves it."

Maybe. But he wasn't ready to tell her yet exactly what he did. And as much as he wanted Cindi all to himself the rest of the week, he realized her adventure needed to get more exciting than just hanging out with him and visiting his mother. As wonderful as it was being around her, it also scared him like hell.

***

She woke the next morning to more gifts. She had enough designer handbags to use a new one every week for a year. If she couldn't find a job, she could certainly raise some cash selling this stuff on eBay.

She unwrapped a beautiful necklace and sighed. Would she have been surrounded by this kind of luxury all her life if her father hadn't died? Would she even have appreciated it? Or would she have become like Gloria, expecting her every whim to be fulfilled?

Setting the necklace aside, she wondered why she wasn't as delighted as she thought she'd be, surrounded by all the items on her dream list.

There was a knock on her door. "It's Henry."

She popped up and let him in, forgetting about the baubles at her feet. Her mood improved immediately seeing him standing there. "Hi! "

He clapped his hands together. "I decided we need to make things more interesting. I'm a boring escort."

She flopped on the sofa in the sitting room. "No, you're perfect."

He shook his head. I contacted a few celebrities interested in spending some time with the girl in the crystal shoes."

"Celebrities? Who?"

"A few singers. Some actors. Everybody wants to hop on the publicity train. But it'll make good highlight clips for us. People don't want to see you hanging out with PR dude from Jiminy shoes. Not when you could be on the arm of an A-lister." He rattled off the names of some very attractive, famous men.

She should be smiling. But hearing your crush read a list of potential dates was a definite buzz kill.

"Do any of them sound good to you?"

No. She wanted more time with him. But clearly he didn't feel the same way if he was so willing to set her up. She had to remember this was just a PR stunt. So, she'd play along as she'd promised.

She looked over his list. Reviewing their names in her head, no one jumped out at her. *This job would be perfect for Gloria, who memorized the pages of* People *like there was going to be a test.* Especially when it came to one guy in particular. A wicked grin spread across her face. Perhaps her stepmother's evil was contagious.

"How about Dirk Jackson?" she offered innocently. She couldn't help smirking, as she imagined Gloria's beady eyes narrowing in anger.

He paused. "That was a quick decision. Okay. I'll set it up."

***

That punk ass good for nothing Oscar nominee Dirk Jackson was way too close to Cindi as they walked down the street, the paparazzi following them. He even had the nerve to tuck a loose strand of hair behind her ear; the very same ear Henry longed to nuzzle and nibble. And the way she smiled up at Dirk hurt worse than a punch to Henry's gut. He was shocked by his reaction. He'd never felt possessive like this over a woman, and certainly not over a woman who wasn't even his.

He tried to find a bad angle from which to shoot Dirk, but there was no such thing as a bad angle of Dirk. He clenched a fist, but reminded himself to calm down. Cindi had been smiling like a fool ever since she'd announced Dirk was the one she wanted. She was enjoying this. This was her week, and it made for good buzz in the press.

And the best part? This was all his fault. He'd suggested this setup, and the boss had loved it.

***

Cindi had done a lot of fake smiling this week. She certainly was having the time of her life, but she was probably the only woman on the planet who could hang out with Dirk Jackson for a few days and not fall in lust. He was gorgeous, of course, and a total gentleman, but she'd liked this whole thing better when it was just her and Henry.

But why torment herself when Henry wasn't interested? He'd admitted his life was all business right now. He'd even cancelled plans with his mother. The man had no time for a personal life. Even so, sometimes, when Dirk was talking to her, she'd find herself sneaking a peek at Henry.

They were out for dinner Thursday night, when Henry dashed off to the restroom. She watched him go, trying to decide if he was six foot one or six foot two.

Dirk turned to her. "You're not really into this, are you?"

She blinked and stammered and basically cranked up her awkward quotient by a thousand. How does a girl answer that question?

He shook his head. "I have women jumping out of the closet in my hotel rooms to get near me. But you?"

He just smiled at her, and lifted a shoulder. "I know. It's him, right?"

"Henry?" She laughed. "No, no, no. Henry? No. He's not looking for a relationship."

He raised one of his thick, trademark eyebrows. "That doesn't mean you're not."

Her lips wobbled like she was a fish out of water; which is exactly how she felt about this whole thing. "Last time I checked, it takes two."

"But, you're okay with us hanging out? I'll be totally honest and tell you it's for the publicity. You know that, right?"

She nodded.

"When Jiminy pitched the idea, my manager insisted. Ticket sales at my last movie weren't great, and he's still miffed I took that bad boy role when I should be concentrating on the romantic leads." He rolled his eyes then fixed his gaze on her. "So, that's why I need to kiss you later tonight."

"Oh?" She blinked at him. "Oh."

"Is that okay?"

She nodded and smiled, thinking of Gloria, locked in her room, kicking the walls like she was still twelve years old after seeing photos of *that*.

"Cool. And just a heads up, once this whole thing is over Saturday night...." He turned up his hands and she knew what he meant. He'd disappear just like the shoes.

"That's fine." She nodded, reassuring him. If only it could be a different ending with Henry, because he'd be disappearing, too. And that thought hurt the most.

Henry rejoined them at the table. "We're all set

with reservations tonight for dinner." He turned to Cindi with a smile. "Your stepmother called her contact at Jiminy looking for tickets to the ball this weekend."

"Ugh." Cindi frowned. "Just be sure to keep her away from me."

"Oh, I lied and told her, 'Tickets are for friends and family only and you seem to be neither.'"

She covered her mouth to hold back what would certainly be an unattractive bellow of laughter.

"Then, after she groveled and whined, I told her I'd check to see if we'd have any left." He shrugged. "Hope you don't mind that I hung up on her when she started screaming. But it's your decision whether you want her there."

"I'd rather have your mother come. I think she'd love to see what you've made of yourself."

He shook his head. "But what should we do about your stepmother?"

She thought about it for a moment. "I might enjoy having her see me there. Gloria, too."

"They don't deserve it, you know. But no swag bag for either of them," he said, calling back the office.

And that's when she knew she was in love.

Too bad her arm was looped around the wrong guy.

***

Just two more days of this nightmare, Henry thought. *Watching the woman you're falling in love with fall in love with someone else, sucks in a thousand different ways*, he thought to himself.

Strolling through the zoo, Dirk stepped aside to make a call.

Cindi sat on a bench and looked up at Henry. "I've

been thinking how we keep talking about how shoes can change a person's life."

"It's true, isn't it?" He sat next to her.

She nodded. "I always thought Jiminies would make me feel like a different person, more important, more fashionable, I don't know. But I still feel like me." She shrugged. "But for some people, shoes really would change their life. I remember donating shoes for some high school project that were shipped to Africa. Some of the kids there didn't even have any shoes."

"There are several projects like that."

"But Jiminy doesn't have one?"

He pursed his lips. "Our designer shoes are hardly appropriate for poor families living in the desert."

She grabbed his arm. "What if you started one, asking each guest to bring an appropriate pair to donate when they come to the ball this weekend? Or by offering customers a discount when they bring a pair of shoes to the store."

He set his hand on hers and stared at her. "I think the boss is going to like this one."

Squeezing his arm, she said, "And maybe you'd feel comfortable inviting your mother to the ball, knowing you're doing something to help others."

A lion roared behind them, and Henry smiled. "Why are you so intent on my mother knowing the truth about my job?"

"I'd do anything to have my mother and father alive. I have to imagine they'd be proud of me no matter what. I think you're robbing the both of you by keeping this a secret."

He grinned at her. "You're a whole lot more than a set of pretty feet, Cindi."

They stared at each other, their hands still linked, when Dirk came back. Henry took his hand away, and Dirk pulled Cindi up from the bench, snaking his arm around her. "Let's hit the reptile house. I kind of miss the cold blooded creatures of Hollywood."

"Just so long as it's not feeding time." She wrinkled her nose. "Poor mice."

Henry shook his head, as he followed behind them. For someone so enthralled with appearances and labels, she really cared about creatures big and small. Even little mice and thirty-something fools like himself. It's not so much that she cared about him; she thought about everyone.

Damn, he was going to miss her when this was all over.

With little enthusiasm, he followed behind them with the camera as they left the zoo. He needed new shots for the latest update on the Jiminy Shoes website. Fans were clamoring for more photos of this budding romance, and he had to feed the publicity machine. Thousands of people had registered to be the next princess for a week. He had no idea there were so many size fives in the world. But none like her.

He had to stop thinking like that. She wasn't his, anymore than those shoes belonged to her. It was a week of magic and that was it. Or at least it had been until Dirk showed up.

Cindi and Dirk were headed for another night of dinner and then dancing at a club. But before they got back in the limo they'd been using, Dirk stopped, wrapped one hand around the back of Cindi's head and pulled her in for a kiss.

He was so stunned, he missed the picture.

And he almost dropped the camera when he saw her huge smile.

Then, it got worse. "Guys, can you do that again? I missed the shot."

Dirk grinned at him. "No problem. I was planning to anyway."

Henry would need his own date later that night to get over this: Captain Morgan, meet Henry Hubbard, the stupidest man in the world.

***

Cindi spent most of Friday choosing the perfect dress for her goodbye ball Saturday night, where she'd part ways with the shoes, and Henry would announce the winner who'd get them next.

Henry was quiet as they went shopping.

"Does this mean you'll be traveling to work with the next shoe girl?" she asked.

"No. There's other publicity work to be done, and there's my mother. We'll find someone else to go. The owner is thrilled how this is unfolding."

Cindi came out of the dressing room in a long, silky blue dress. "Does this look alright?"

He could only nod.

"Okay. I'll get it. Can we stop and get some chocolate before I head back to the hotel?"

"Why?"

"I'm going to need a load of it for Sunday morning when it's back to the real world."

He set his hand on her bare shoulder and willed himself not to let it wander to other more interesting locations. "It's not going to be your old world. Trust me, with the coverage you've gotten you're going to get other offers." And then there's Dirk, who didn't seem to be

37

going anywhere soon. "This isn't over for you yet."

Just for us, it is.

He'd never tried chocolate therapy, but maybe he'd stock up on some, too.

***

Cindi truly felt like a princess as she got dressed Saturday night. A hair and makeup artist had been sent to get her ready. A horse and carriage waited outside the hotel to drive her to the farewell party. Dirk had stashed champagne and roses in the carriage, which he presented to her after she climbed in—with another kiss. For a fake kiss, it was not bad at all.

As the carriage pulled away, she waved to Henry standing on the sidewalk, taping the whole thing. Her heart sank as the horse pranced away from the man she would've rather spent the evening with.

When they arrived at the hotel, the paparazzi were lined up outside ready for her walk down the red carpet. "Show us the shoes!" they cried as she descended from the carriage.

She lifted the hem of her long dress, exposing her foot for the camera.

Dirk paused to kiss her hand, and then led her along the walkway. Cameras flashed like the Fourth of July on steroids. She walked into the ballroom, beautifully decorated with candles and white roses. Big tables were set up with collection bins for people to donate their shoes. A crowd was already gathered inside, and her stomached dropped when she saw her stepmother and Gloria rushing toward her and Henry walked in and gave Cindi a look. "I'm on it. Go enjoy yourself, Cindi."

Dirk led her to the dance floor, and while she

didn't know how to waltz, he did a fine job leading the way.

"When the press asks why we aren't together anymore, what are you going to say?" Cindi asked. It's not that she'd miss him, but she didn't want to be humiliated.

His big hands squeezed hers. "I'm going to fly out to the west coast and meet with some directors. I figure we'll just let this fizzle out. Sound okay with you?"

"Sounds good."

"Under different circumstances, I think something could've happened between us," he said.

Not if she'd met Henry first. "Yeah, maybe."

The song came to an end and he dipped her. Then he brought her back up, and nuzzled her cheek. "I didn't expect to have so much fun with you this week. And you've really helped get me back in the papers. I hate that this is part of the job, but it is what it is. Thanks for everything."

"Hey, don't think I got nothing out of this. My stepsister will be jealous for the rest of her life." She looked over where Henry had Gloria and her stepmother corralled in a corner table. Gloria waved to her, and Cindi responded by kissing Dirk.

Too bad Henry had seen it as well.

Dirk looked over at them. "I hope you get your guy."

"Can't have everything," Cindi said. "Certainly not at the same time." The shoes certainly seemed magical, but they weren't perfect.

"I'm going to work the room. We'll catch up before midnight," he said, his hand slipping from hers.

Cindi wanted to talk with Henry, but she was swept

away on the dance floor by guest after guest. She was nearly held captive in the ladies room by a woman with wild, blond curls who was dying to know what Dirk was really like and if he needed an apartment sitter.

"Have him call me. Goldie Lockston," she made the universal call me sign, holding pinky to mouth and thumb to ear while passing Cindi a card.

When she left the restroom, she spotted Henry dancing with an older woman. There was no mistaking her big, brown eyes; she'd been staring at them on Henry's face for a week now. She hurried over, unable to hold back a huge grin.

He stopped dancing and smiled. "Cindi, this is my mother, Nancy Hubbard. Mom, this is Cindi."

They shook hands. "So nice to meet you. What do you think of all this? Your son is a marketing genius."

His mother squeezed his arm. "I'm so proud. I can't believe he works for such a high falutin' company and was keeping it a secret." Then she whacked him with her purse. "And all of these years I could have had the most stylish shoes in town." She lifted her foot. "My first pair of Jiminies. Don't you love them?"

"They're fabulous." She smiled at Henry, and felt her heart melt for him seeing him so pleased. "And did you see he's collecting shoes for the needy?"

"I'm not surprised. Henry looks out for everyone." She put her hand on his cheek. "But my son needs to start looking out for himself, too. Now excuse me, I want to chase down that Dirk fellow for a dance."

Then another guest tapped Cindi's shoulder. As the man pulled her away, Henry caught her hand. "I'm sorry, we were just about to dance."

Henry swirled her across the floor for several songs

as the orchestra played several favorite classical tunes. *If only the night could end like this,* she thought. *In Henry's arms.*

But duty called, and Henry led her off the dance floor. "You're wonderful, Cindi." And he walked away. Which was the exact opposite of being in his arms, she noted. Her wishes weren't coming true anymore; this whole thing was really ending.

After that, she had more glasses of champagne than she could count, posed for more pictures than she had in the past ten years, and smiled so much her face hurt. Then before she knew it, the giant clock set up inside specifically for the party chimed fifteen minutes before midnight.

Her heart sank. This whirlwind was coming to an end. And in some ways she was grateful. It would be nice not to worry what her butt looked like every time Henry was behind her filming. And honestly, it would be wonderful to wear another pair of shoes. But as she looked across the room at Henry, talking on his cell phone, while directing the press to the stage where Cindi would turn over her shoes, her stomach kerplunked like a coin in a well that didn't stand a chance of granting its wish. Or like a coin in the fountain they'd had installed right there in the ballroom for partygoers to make their own wishes. Not far from the white horse people could pose next to for a keepsake photo. And who could forget the incredible cupcake display? They'd even made sure there were some healthy options for people into that kind of thing. A pumpkin seed muffin? The Sea Goddess muffin? People would be talking about this party for a long time.

She felt a hand slide around her waist. "Ready for our last dance?" Dirk's voice was deep and sultry and she wondered what was wrong with her for not feeling attracted to him.

But they had to keep up the charade, so she nodded, and Dirk led her to the dance floor. He spun her and dipped her as the crowd oohed and ahhed and the cameras rolled. Then, with a few minutes left until midnight, he escorted up her on stage, where she sat on a beautiful marble bench. He stepped aside as Henry approached her, wearing a clip-on wireless microphone.

"Cindi, your magical week is coming to an end. At Jiminy Shoes, we like to say shoes can change your life, and indeed, they changed yours."

She looked up at him and nodded, blinking back the tears. She wished it was just the two of them there, and she could kick off the shoes without a second thought and fold herself into his arms.

Henry slid off the first shoe. The lights on the stage dimmed; the candles on the table were blown out. The place was whisper quiet and she got goose bumps from the drama of it all. When he took off the second shoe, the spotlight on her went out. The room was in total darkness.

One of his assistants escorted Cindi backstage. Then the lights came back on and Henry was announcing the next lucky woman to wear the enchanted shoes. Someone in Sweden. Probably a supermodel so beautiful he'd be willing to make his first international trip.

She decided she'd let herself pout for a day or two, then she'd work to parlay the media attention into more business for herself. The Princess Party Planner? The Best Foot Forward Event Planner? She'd come up with something. But for now, she was crashing like a chocoholic coming off the sugar high of a lifetime.

***

As the party guests filed out of the ballroom, Henry watched Cindi wander over to the fountain and toss in a coin. She sat on the edge gazing at the water.

Despite the publicists waiting outside for him hoping to set their clients up with the next crystal shoe girl, he went to her. "If you wished for another week with the shoes, I can't make it happen. Sorry."

She looked up at him. "No, I'm fine." She scrubbed the heel of her hand across her cheek. Shit, she'd been crying.

He sat next to her. "I'm sorry. I didn't realize this would be so hard on you. You can come pick out all the shoes you want tomorrow. I promise."

She laughed through her tears. "A week ago that would have been a dream come true."

"But it's not now?"

She shook her head.

He opened the box he'd been carrying with him. "Here, while no one's looking, wear them one last time." He handed her the shoes and she set them in her lap.

"Thanks," she whispered, but didn't move to put them on.

"Ah, so it's not that either. It's problems with Dirk, then. Was he just after your feet?" He hoped he sounded funnier than he felt.

She laughed. "No, just after publicity."

He gritted his teeth. "You sure? You two seemed pretty interested in each other." He was still trying to erase their kisses from his mind.

"I was just trying to annoy my stepsister, and he was just trying to get in the tabloids. It worked."

His heart surged. Was she truly not interested in one

of the hottest guys in Hollywood? "And now?"

She shrugged. "It's over. That's all it ever was. He was totally upfront with me about it. And I told him I wasn't interested either."

He was relieved, but confused. "So, what's bothering you so much you came over here to make a wish? You had everything this week. What more could you wish for?"

She closed her eyes. "Now I have to find a job and a new place to live."

Ah. He had to make this right for her. Maybe what his mother had said was true, he did worry about people. But Cindi was worth worrying over. "Don't think twice about a job. We'd be smart to have you working in one of our stores. People would come in just to see you. We can get you a job for now. But you deserve something better. And I'll see that you have another week in the hotel so you can find a place to live. Is that what's making you so sad?"

She looked up at him. "I thought the clothes and shoes and all the attention would be a dream come true. It's what I've always wanted. It reminded me of when I was little and my father showered me with gifts. This week was great, really." She frowned. "At first anyway. But then I realized what I really missed was the time spent with my father, not the stuff he got me. And now, I'm going to miss the time I spent with you." She looked down at the shoes in her lap, running her fingers along the heels.

He stared at her. "You're going to miss me?"

She nodded. "I guess the timing's just wrong. I know you're not looking for a girlfriend right now. You're focused on your career. I get that. And now you're going to be busier than ever. It's over."

He reached for her hand, but his mother picked the perfect time to wander over. "So, I suppose you'll be going to Sweden to work with the next shoe girl?"

"No, don't worry, Mother. I'll be here for you."

She waved off the idea with a white-gloved hand. "Too bad you couldn't go. You should see some of the world instead of doting on me. You need to get yourself a nice girl. I won't be around forever. And besides, I have a gentleman friend in town. The butcher, who is going to love these new shoes." She waggled her eyebrows. "And the baker I've been seeing on the side might like them, too. Now where'd all those waiters with the champagne go?" She wandered off looking for another drink.

Cindi grabbed his arms. "Henry, you should go to Sweden."

"You don't want me here?"

She widened her eyes; her lovely, green eyes. "I don't want you to miss any more of your life."

He pursed his lips and looked up at the ceiling. Then he looked back at her. "Do you have a passport?"

She nodded.

"Let me make a phone call." He walked across the room so Cindi couldn't hear the conversation. Once he got the owner of Jiminy on the line, Henry got the answers he was hoping for.

"What do you think about coming to Sweden with me? You're the new director of our Do Good Shoe Good project."

She looked up at him and tossed the shoes aside. He picked her up and swung her around. Then he swept his lips across hers, until the plump pout of her lower lip was tucked between his in a delicious kiss. "So, you're not upset about not being a princess anymore?"

"I feel like a princess now. That wishing well of yours worked."

He wrapped his arms around her and held her against him. They fit together like a perfect pair of shoes. It was probably too soon to tell her, but the owner of Jiminy Shoes had promised the crystal heels would belong to Cindi for good when she and Henry got married. Henry smiled as he was kissing her, just thinking of it.

"What?" she asked, between kisses.

"I always wondered what happily ever after felt like."

"Red"
by Lisa Scott

Rose had four-dozen pumpkin seed muffins left over from the Shoe Ball the night before along with three-dozen Sea Goddess muffins. They hadn't been quite the hit she'd hoped. She hung the closed sign in the window and grabbed her basket of leftovers. Seemed like Grandma Kate was the only one benefiting from her floundering bakery. Rose couldn't bear to toss out the leftovers at the end of the day, so she often stopped by Grandma's on the way home to share the goodies. The lease on Yum Yum Good For You was up in three months, and she'd probably have to close the shop. She couldn't argue with the numbers on the balance sheet, but it cleaved her heart in two just thinking of it. At age twenty-five, she hadn't found success yet in her personal life or her professional life. The word "failure" nipped at the edges of her sleep every night.

She slipped on her long, red cape and stepped outside into the chilly night. Wearing such a bright color increased her chances of grabbing a cab by fifty percent—she'd done several informal comparisons to back up her theory. Her red cape had become her thing and she now owned three in different styles and never had to worry about a ride. Sure, it clashed with her hair, but so what?

The second cab she spotted pulled over to pick her up. "Where to?" asked the driver.

"Grimm Towers, over on Sherwood Street."

He whistled. "Swanky."

"Oh, I don't live there. My grandmother does."

No, Rose had a tiny studio downtown. It was cozy and cheap. If the bakery folded she couldn't exactly downsize her digs. Anything smaller than her apartment would be considered a roomy closet. Quite a difference from the rambling farmhouse she grew up in out in the country.

She pulled back the checkered cloth covering her basket. "Can I interest you in a free pumpkin seed muffin? It's made with spelt flour, oats, bran, and organic pumpkins, topped with pumpkin seeds. I own the bakery back there."

The cabbie looked at her in the rear view mirror, wrinkling his big nose. "Got a cupcake? I could really go for a cupcake."

She let out a long sigh. More than one customer had wandered into her shop—only to make a quick exit when they didn't spot any cupcakes or gooey treats. She'd been so certain there was a market for her healthy baked goods. After her mother died from a heart attack, she'd been determined to give the world better food choices. Maybe it would've helped her mother; Rose owed her that.

Her bakery offered it all: gluten-free, casein-free, vegan, and multi-grain breads, muffins, and buns. The recent seaweed trend inspired her new Sea Goddess Muffin. It hadn't caught on yet. Hopefully Grandma Kate would like them; she had quite a few in her basket. Perhaps Rose would tell her they were pistachio muffins instead.

She rubbed her thumb over the ridges on her basket, trying to soothe her nerves. What was she going to do if the bakery closed? She had no idea, but she needed to come up with a plan soon. She'd been shocked when Jiminy Shoes contacted her about showcasing her goods.

She'd hoped the Shoe Ball would bring some new clients, but not so much. Her baked good had remained untouched next to the cupcakes and desserts. Barring some lottery win or wish on a star, her bakery would be history. Her pity party consumed the rest of the ride and finally, the cab came to a stop. "We're here already?"

"Yep. Over the river and through the woods. Well, past Sherwood park, anyway."

"Thanks." Always the marketer, she gave him her card. "Just in case you change your mind about healthy muffins. A daily serving of oats can reduce your cholesterol by ten percent, you know."

"Uh, thanks, but I'm going to grab a pizza and take my chances with a slice of sausage and double cheese."

Sausage and cheese had been her mother's favorite. She was fairly certain her mother had never eaten bran in any shape or form. After paying the driver, she took the elevator up to the 55th floor, rang her grandmother's doorbell and stepped back. Swinging her basket back and forth, she waited. And waited. And waited.

Rose studied the square-toed, low-heeled shoes she'd stuffed her feet into that morning and frowned. She felt like a frump compared to all the glamorous people the night before.

She rang the bell again. What was taking her Grandmother so long? A nervous feeling left her hands shaking. She couldn't lose Grandma, too. Her mother had passed two years ago; Rose couldn't take another tragedy. She pounded the door with her fist. "Grandma?"

"I'm coming, I'm coming," her grandmother said on the other side of the door.

49

Rose let out a long breath once she heard her voice.

The heavy door opened and Rose blinked at her Grandmother. Her heart rate picked up again. "Are you okay, Grandma Kate?" Grandma's face was flushed and a sheen of perspiration covered her forehead. Grandma spent an hour every morning applying full makeup— eyebrow pencil, lip liner, false eyelashes—then tried on at least a dozen outfits before settling on the perfect one for the day: a casual pantsuit for a trip to the market, a form-fitting dress for the charity luncheon, smart business wear when she attended to her business affairs. Yet there she stood in her doorway with her hair out of place, much of her make up worn off, and wrapped up in a silky golden robe.

Rose reached for her arm. "Are you sick? What's going on?" Fear tied itself into a knot in her belly. Or maybe it was the parsnip bread she'd made earlier. That hadn't turned out so well.

Grandma led her inside. "I'm not sick. In fact, I've never felt better."

That's when Rose noticed a man putting on a black wool coat in the living room. A man of the tall-dark-and-handsome variety. And young. Much younger than her grandmother. Under his coat, he was dressed casually, in loose pants and a turtleneck. Was he a neighbor, maybe? Someone from the building co-cop asking Grandma to keep her holiday decorations off her door? Even Rose thought the Valentine's wreath covered with cupids that resembled drunk, naked babies was a bit tacky.

The man gave Rose the once over. Suddenly, her shoes seemed real interesting. She looked up at Grandma with wide, worried eyes—which flicked over to the strapping young man who widened his stance and crossed his arms. What was he doing, staking his claim?

Cricket trotted out and sat at his feet, looking up at him adoringly. Her jaw dropped. That little pooch didn't like anyone.

Grandma gave Rose an odd look, then walked over to the man and hugged him. She tipped up on her toes and whispered in his ear. His eyebrows shot up, then he shrugged and nodded. Grandma giggled. Her grandmother *giggled*. "Thanks, Jack. That was wonderful." Her cheeks flushed an even deeper shade of pink.

"You were great," he answered.

Rose's mouth dropped open again. She looked back and forth between her grandmother, and this man, with his blue eyes, big muscles, and self-assured smile. Scratch that, it wasn't a smile—it was a smirk. He was smirking at Grandma Kate! And you only smirk if you have something to smirk about.

Then Grandma smirked back at him. Heck, even Cricket seemed to be smirking. *Oh, my organic bran rolls.* Was Grandma having an affair?

Grandma broke their embrace and eyed Rose's basket. "I'm starving. What've you got in here?"

Rose couldn't take her gaze of the man looking possessively at her grandmother. "Uh, Sea Goddess muffins and a few pumpkin seed muffins."

Her grandmother sighed. "I could really use a cupcake after … that."

The basket slipped from Rose's grip and thudded onto the floor.

"Did I tell you, Jack, my granddaughter owns the Yum Yum Good For You Bakery?"

"You didn't." His voice was deep and gravelly—just like an illicit lover's voice should be. "A bakery that's good for you? That doesn't sound very exciting." He walked over and picked up her basket, inspecting the contents.

Rose planted her hands on her hips. "Some people care about what they eat."

He reached into the basket and pulled out a Sea Goddess Muffin. "What big muffins you have. I'd be interested in the calorie count of this versus a cupcake. Maybe they're not so healthy after all."

Huh. She had no idea how many calories were in her muffins. She was more interested in providing healthy ingredients. She tipped up her chin. "I'll find out and let you know."

He looked her up and down in a way that made her feel like she'd forgotten a key article of clothing that morning—even though she was still wrapped in her cape. "Good." He turned his attention to Grandma. "So, I'll see you Thursday, Kate?"

She winked at him. Winked! "I'll be looking forward to it."

Then he pointed at Rose. "And I hope to see you later, Red."

"It's Rose."

"Nope. With hair and a cape like that, you're Red to me."

The nerve of him making up a nickname for her. She'd just met him! What kind of guy does that? "That's nervy. You don't even know me."

"Oh, that's just his way. He calls me Kitten," Grandma said.

Rose started coughing and spotted empty wine glasses on the marble coffee table in the living room. She couldn't even find the words to demand an explanation;

not that one was needed. Grandma was having an affair with this—this big, handsome player. Wasn't there a knitting circle for her to join? Shouldn't she have an elderly gentleman friend who smelled like olives and enjoyed bocce? You know, an appropriate boyfriend for a grandmother? Someone who would call her ma'am instead of kitten?

But then again, Grandma didn't exactly look like someone's old nana. She was just sixty-six, but she still wore her hair in a beautiful honey-blond bob, fit into her size four designer suits and never left her home if she wasn't fully made up and wearing fabulous shoes. And Rose didn't know for sure, but Grandma Kate most likely did not wear granny panties. All that, and she still had a smoking hot figure.

The man standing in her apartment was admiring that as well. Knowing she was loaded probably didn't hurt either. He swaggered past them, and kissed Grandma's hand while smiling at Rose.

Her eyes widened and she strapped her arms across her chest. When he finally let himself out the door—with the Sea Goddess muffin—Rose turned to her grandmother. "What was that?" she managed to ask.

Grandma blinked at her, suppressing a smile. "Don't you mean '*Who* was that' dear?"

Rose turned up her hands. "Yes, who was that and what was he doing here and what's with all the smirking and winking and giggling?"

"That was Jack Wolff and I'm sure you can figure out what he was doing here." Grandma plucked the wine glasses off the table and headed for the kitchen with a swing to her hips.

Wolff. That sounded right. On wobbly knees, Rose

plopped down on the couch. "But … but … he's so young."

Grandma looked over her shoulder at her and waggled her eyebrows. "I know. He's perfect for the job."

Job? Oh, sweet berry muffins, she's paying him. "Why?"

Grandma drifted back into the room and sat in a chair across from Rose. "Darling, I really need it at my age. You know what it's like."

Rose's mouth opened and closed as she tried to protest. "I'm not really part of that scene any more." Sure, she'd had the boyfriend of the month for a while. But that was before, when she staggered in at all hours of the night, drinking and basically making her mother's life a living hell. Everything was different now that Mom was gone.

Grandma leaned toward her. "Plus, he's got the biggest—"

"Gosh, the weather's been cold, huh?" Rose stood up, interrupting, so she wouldn't have to wash out her ears later from their conversation. "Snow and sleet and freezing rain. And the barometer's been falling…"

Grandma sighed. "Sweetheart, I'd really love to chat, but I'm exhausted and I need a shower. We'll catch up later this week, alright?"

"Umm … yes. Of course. Right." She gathered her things and headed for the door in a daze. She and Grandma usually chatted for hours while watching classic movies on cable, selecting an incredible wine from Grandma's collection to go with the show, and usually ignoring her goodies from the bakery, now that she thought about it. "Well, bye, Grandma."

"Wait, Rose!"

Thank goodness. Grandma was going to sit her down and explain everything. Rose turned around, hopeful. "Yes?"

Grandma dashed to the door with her basket. "Don't forget these. I think those green ones have gone bad. They smell like low tide down at the pier."

Rose grabbed the basket and she was so distracted, she left the building without her cape.

Five cabs passed her before she got a ride.

***

When Rose got home, she spent an hour checking the calorie contents on all the ingredients in her muffins. Then adding up the total—and adding again. "Six-hundred fifty calories?" she whispered to herself. But still, they were six hundred fifty calories of good, healthy ingredients. What made her even more upset, though, was that Jack had been right.

Jack. The name made her shudder just remembering his deep blue eyes, his bulging biceps, and entrancing smile. At least she thought the feeling was a shudder, because it would be really wrong to have any lustful thoughts for her grandma's *lover*. She wondered how much she was paying him. Where'd she find him anyway? She had no idea how such an arrangement worked.

Curiosity was killing her, so she called Grandma, hoping she wasn't asleep yet. Grandma answered on the third ring. "Rose, what is it? Did you get sick from one of those green muffins?"

"No. I was curious. Where did you meet Jack?"

"Facebook. He has a fan page celebrating older women. Good night, darling."

Rose was woozy with shock as she sat in the corner of her apartment that served as her kitchen. Once she came back to her senses, she slammed her cookbook on the table. He had a Facebook page luring in seniors? He was a predator. Should she put a stop to this?

With a sigh, she slumped in her chair. No, she had to leave this be. It wasn't her place. Grandma seemed happy and she knew what she was doing. At least someone in her family did, because Rose certainly didn't.

***

Rose spent the next morning looking for ways to reduce the calorie count in her muffins. She replaced the olive oil in the Sea Goddess muffins with applesauce, and was pleased with the test batch.

She filled the display case with the muffins, trying to ignore the fact she hadn't had a customer in twenty-two minutes. She always got nervous when half an hour had passed without a sale. She needed to sell just over five hundred-fifty dollars worth of goods a day, so on average, she needed to make twenty three-dollars in sales every thirty minutes. She wasn't going to give up on this place. She'd be fighting for her business to the bitter end.

Cutting up one of the muffins, she placed a few samples of Bran Apple Betty on the counter. The bell on the door jangled and she let out the breath she'd been holding. A customer. She'd make sure they bought something, even if she had to offer a half-price discount. Smiling, she looked up.

The knife slipped from her fingers and hit the floor, which was probably for the best; Jack was standing in her store, grinning.

"What are you doing here?"

"Looking for another Sea Goddess muffin. It was good. I felt energized after I ate it last night. At least, I think it was the muffin that left me feeling that way." One arrogant eyebrow popped up.

She pursed her lips. "I'm all out. And you were right. The muffins are high in calories."

He walked toward her and leaned against the counter. "So make them smaller." He smiled at her and darn her heart for kicking up a notch.

"That's what I'd been planning to do," she lied, although it was a good idea. She crossed her arms. "Are you seeing my grandmother today?"

"She wanted to, but I'm booked up. Maybe tomorrow."

"Don't you think she's a little old for you?"

He widened his stance and crossed his arms. "She's perfect for me. My specialty, actually."

She sucked in a breath and couldn't get the words out.

"I'll take a dozen Sea Goddess muffins. Looks like you've got some right here in the display case."

"Oh. Right." She thought about not serving him. But his sale would mean she'd break her half hour curse. Reluctantly, she filled his order, rang up the sale and handed him the box of muffins. "Thank you."

His eyes twinkled. "You're just as beautiful as your grandmother. Must be the health benefits of your goodies." He handed her two twenties.

Snatching the money, she gritted her teeth and bit back a thousand nasty things she could say. Is this how the exchange happened with Grandma Kate? A handful of twenties passed over when they were all done? Or was it hundreds? "Please don't hurt my grandmother." She made change and slammed the cash register drawer shut.

"We're careful. She won't get hurt." He glanced

over his shoulder as he left the shop. "Don't you ever do anything for fun, Red?"

She planted her hands on her hips. "No, I do not. I work too hard."

"Have a little fun, Red. Go bake a cupcake." One side of his mouth curled up and he left.

"It's Rose!" she shouted after him. She waited a few seconds and then dashed to the window to see where he was going. With her palms against the glass, she swore. A woman in a long fur coat was kissing him on the cheek.

That's it. She grabbed her cloak, locked the door, and dashed down the street. She had to find that woman and get the goods on Jack.

"Excuse me! Ma'am? Wait!" Rose chased after the woman, but a cab pulled up to the sidewalk and the woman climbed in.

Rose was breathless as she watched the cab pull away. *How'd she get a cab so quickly—without a red cape?*

"Is there something I can help you with?"

She spun around and saw Jack leaning against a building.

"Who was that woman?"

He pushed away from the building and walked towards her. "Who?"

"The one who just got in a cab. The one who kissed you!"

He cocked his head and smiled at her. "That was one of my mother's friends."

She exhaled in surprise.

"I'm seeing her later tonight."

Rose pursed her lips, made a grumpy, dismissive noise, and spun around. She marched back to her shop, fished her keys out of her apron pocket, opened the door, and called her grandmother.

"Rose, you're turning into a pesky old lady. What is it?"

"You can't see Jack again."

"What?"

"I just saw another woman kissing him on the street."

Grandma laughed. "Rose, I know I'm not the only one."

Right. Of course. *Gigolos have lots of women.* "Aren't there any nice men in your building?"

"Oh yes, there's a prince up in the penthouse," Grandma said.

Rose pinched the bridge of her nose. "Grandma, seriously…."

"What? There is, from some tiny European country. But rumor has it he's a beast. A nasty, nasty man. I like Jack. I'm a grown woman, Rose. I know what I'm doing."

The idea of turning Jack in to the police crossed her mind, but then Grandma would get in trouble, too. Who was the John, here? Grandma or Jack? What did it matter? Grandma was going to do what she wanted. "Okay, fine. I just hope you don't get hurt."

"We're being careful."

Making a face, Rose hung up, and swore she heard Grandma giggling. Well, if Jack was making her happy and making her feel young again, who was she to break up that kind of magic? He was her fountain of youth, apparently. She'd have to grit her teeth and be nice. And try to forget that Jack was the most gorgeous man Rose had ever seen.

Who happened to be sleeping with her grandmother.

Whoever said life was unfair was absolutely right.

***

Jack was there again when Rose dropped off flax seed cookies on Thursday. Grandma peeked in the basket and frowned. "Rose, dear, I do appreciate the gesture, but I'm not interested in your tofu cookies and multi-grain breads. When you start making cinnamon sticky buns and chocolate torte, you can drop off all you like. Though I doubt you'd have any left."

She stood up straight. "Grandma, you know I'm all about healthy choices, now."

"And I'm into indulgence now." Her voice was low and sultry.

"You could learn a few things from Kate," Jack said, looking gorgeous in a pale blue sweater and jeans. He kissed Grandma's hand, and whispered, "Should we tell her?"

Panic walloped Rose's chest. "Tell me what?"

"Nothing darling. Nothing you need to know yet." She shared a knowing look with Jack.

He just shrugged. "Okay, then. You're in charge. It's your call, Kate."

Oh, my mammoth zucchini muffin. Are they going on vacation? Getting married? With just a little bit of Grandma's money, Jack wouldn't have to hustle so many other old ladies. That's probably what he was thinking. Grandma wasn't just a senior cougar; no, this was much worse.

Rose jerked her thumb over her shoulder. "I'm going to go." She had no choice but to tolerate this; but that didn't mean she had to watch it.

"Bye, darling," Grandma said, never taking her eyes off Jack.

***

She got to the bakery before the sun was up the next morning. She hadn't been able to sleep, and there were numbers to review and muffins to make. Wanting to please her calorie conscious customers, she was going to offer different sized muffins and list the calories and ingredients for all her goods, along with the benefits of the select ingredients. She hated that Jack had inspired this new strategy, but then again, even gigolos needed good marketing skills to get ahead.

She dumped a cup of rice flour in a mixing bowl. With Valentine's Day approaching, she wanted to experiment with some romantic treats. A rose hip bread would be nice. She stirred some dried cherries into the mix. The rose hips were said to soothe the nerves and cherries aroused desire in women. Passion Bread, that's what she would call it. That might be appealing to her clients. She wouldn't let her grandmother have any of it, though. When the first batch cooled, she sunk her teeth into the warm, moist bread. She smiled. It was good.

The hours flew by—she had another piece of bread—and she flipped her sign to 'open' right before seven a.m. She didn't have to wait long for her first customer to arrive. When the bells jingled, she looked up and frowned—while running a hand down her hip and then smoothing her hair. She shouldn't have had that second piece of passion bread. She blew out her breath. "So, you finished all your muffins already?"

"I've been sharing them with my clients. It keeps up their stamina," Jack said.

It probably did. Seaweed detoxified the body and increased metabolism. It also helped with impotence—a problem he certainly didn't have. She pointed a wooden spoon at him. "Do not talk to me about the other women in your life and what you're doing with them." She shivered as an image of her grandmother wearing a silk teddy and feather boa popped into her brain.

His big lips curled into that darn smile of his and she closed her eyes to keep it from affecting her, too.

"I'm just doing what your grandmother wants. There's a lot you don't understand about our relationship." Her eyes popped open and he stepped closer to her and leaned against the counter. "Give me a chance. I'm not as bad as you think."

Rose backed away from him.

He laughed. "Are you afraid of me?"

"Of course not."

"I'm hardly the big bad wolf, Rose. So, are you going to serve me?"

Well, butter my croissant. Is that how it worked? Grandma was the one who did all the…. She shook the thought from her head and blinked at him.

"Your muffin."

Rose blinked at him again. Exactly what was he proposing?

"The Seafood Goddess muffin. Can I have two dozen of the small ones? They are for sale, right?"

"Oh, yeah. Yes, of course that's what you meant. I'll get those right away." She wiped away the line of perspiration beading above her lip. She needed to create a literal humble pie. Or a deep dish pie of common sense. What would be good for that—ginger?

"I like these. I usually don't go for health food stuff. But these are good," he said, tapping the display case.

"Thank you," she said tersely, handing him the

box.

He grabbed a few cards stacked up in a clear acrylic box by the register. "I'm going to pass these out to my clients. I'm going to recommend they bulk up on a muffin before I arrive."

She didn't know what to say. Would that make her some sort of accessory to this whole sordid thing?

"Hey, if you stop by Kate's tonight, bring some of that pink bread in there. It looks good."

"If there's any left." Which there would not be. Neither of them would be getting any passion bread. She'd give them something absolutely unsexy, like licorice. She frowned. Licorice actually had tons of health food benefits. She'd have to whip up something with a bit of it mixed in.

Maybe she wouldn't stop by at all. Maybe Grandma didn't even want her visiting anymore. Rose had assumed Grandma could use the company and would enjoy some left over baked goods. *She doesn't need me or my vegan banana bread when she's got a hot, fresh, stud muffin.*

But she couldn't turn a blind eye to this nonsense. She was going to keep visiting. Maybe she could guilt grandma into giving up her escort. *Maybe I need to visit even more often.*

Jack smiled at her before leaving and she hated the feeling of lust that curled inside her. Guess he just had that kind of effect on everyone. Grandma didn't stand a chance.

The cab fares were killing her, but what if Jack was out to swindle her Grandma? Being a sugar granny was one thing. But Jack could very well clear out Grandma's sizeable bank account. She couldn't afford not to go for another visit.

***

That night, Grandma was in the shower when she arrived. *Well, at least they're not in there together*, she thought. She sat down on the couch with a sigh.

Jack tossed the magazine he'd been reading onto the table. "So, looking to join us for some fun, Red?"

Her mouth opened and closed and she finally managed to say, "Excuse me?"

"While I specialize in older women, I do have clients of all ages. We could make an arrangement. Your baked goods for my services."

She popped up from her seat and went to the kitchen for a drink. She hadn't had alcohol since her mother died, but she might kill Jack if she didn't calm down. A nice Riesling usually did the trick. "I am not interested in any business dealings with you."

He followed her into the kitchen, and she downed the entire glass of wine. "Were you always like this?" she asked. She could imagine him pimping himself out as a prom date to girls across the city.

"You mean, generous enough to share my gifts with those in need?" His eyes locked on hers and she looked away.

"Yes, generous, that's how I'd describe you."

"Actually, I wanted to be a doctor. But in college, I realized this line of business was better suited for me."

"It's always good to find that perfect career match."

"What about you? Did you always want to be a baker?"

She laughed. "No. I had no idea what I wanted to do. But I knew I had to get my act together after my mother died and baking was one of the few things I enjoyed doing. It was either that or party for a living, and Paris Hilton had that socialite thing all tied up at the time."

He leaned against the counter and she could smell a whiff of mesmerizing aftershave. He stared at her long enough that it made her uncomfortable and she found herself crossing her arms. He chuckled. "Oh, so you did know how to have fun once upon a time."

"I had enough fun for a lifetime."

Grandma breezed into the kitchen in a new, silky kimono. *Good grape seed streusel.* What had these two been getting up to? Is that whole Kama Sutra thing Japanese? Is that what this was?

"Now, Rose, you're not trying to steal away Jack from me, are you?"

She shook her head so hard it hurt.

"I'm sure he could fit you in, too."

Holy whole-wheat bagels. "I'm going to get going. I left some muffins for you guys on the table."

"If it's the money, Rose, I can pay for it! Jack's expensive but he's worth it," Grandma hollered after her.

There really wasn't any amount of wine that could erase that comment from her memory bank.

***

The next morning, Rose was at work, beating a bowl full of eggs much harder than necessary. Now they were too frothy for her recipe. She dumped them down the sink and sighed. She had to stop this relationship. That, or she had to stop seeing Grandma for a while. Rose was more and more upset each time she visited. *This must be my punishment for putting my mother through such hell all those years.* She cringed, remembering the time she dragged home a guy from Germany in the middle of the night who spoke no English at all. Her mother spent an hour staring at him in the kitchen the next morning offering him eggs and pancakes and toast until she finally shook Rose awake.

When she closed up shop that night, she decided this would be her last visit to Grandma's. She was going to lay it on the line: *leave Jack or lose me.* She bundled up her goodies and her determination, and headed uptown.

Clutching her basket of banana buns in front of her, she rang Grandma's doorbell. This time, Jack answered the door. "Hello, Red."

She was constantly rolling her eyes around this guy. "Where's my grandmother?"

"Why don't you come in?"

He was acting like he owned the place; he was probably imagining he did.

Squeezing past him, since he was blocking most of the doorway with his broad shoulders and thick thighs—thighs that she tried so hard not to look at—she called for her grandmother. "It's me, Grandma. I've got something new for you to try."

Jack nodded. "Your grandmother likes to try new things."

Rose clenched her teeth and counted to ten under her breath. Luckily, Grandma breezed out of her bedroom, dressed in her kimono again. Rose wasn't sure if there was anything under that kimono. The thought made her shudder. Which was why she had to do this.

"Grandma, we need to talk."

"Of course, dear." Grandma walked over to Jack and set her hand on his shoulder, leaning against him. "Want to know what we've been doing?"

"No, please, I don't want the specifics."

Grandma shrugged. "We'll show you then."

Rose dropped her basket and covered her eyes.

"No! Don't show me, for the love of lavender biscuits." Rose heard the rustle of Grandma's robe as she tried to back up toward the door with her eyes still closed.

"Lavender biscuits. Now those sound lovely," Grandma said, dreamily.

"Okay, on all fours, Kate," Jack said.

A whimper slipped out Rose's lips.

"Oh, I'm too sore for that, darling."

Rose whacked her heel on Grandma's credenza as she tried to blindly flee the apartment. She reached and grabbed around her, trying to get her bearings.

"Okay, let's start on your back, Kate," Jack said.

"Hold my ankles, then."

Rose tripped over the rug and landed on her butt, but even worse—she opened her eyes. "What are you two doing?" She looked back and forth between Jack and her Grandmother. *They're still clothed.* Jack held Grandma's ankles while she did—"Sit ups?" Rose asked, incredulously.

"I believe they're called crunches these days," Grandma said.

"Yep, that's what most of my clients call them," Jack confirmed.

Rose scrambled to her feet, heart pounding. "Wait, so you're not … I mean, you two aren't …because I thought…."

One corner of Jack's mouth quirked up. "Oh, I know what you thought."

Rose stomped her foot. "Why did you let me believe that?"

He shrugged and shook his head. "Ask your Grandma. It was her idea."

"Grandma?" Her words came out in a raspy

whisper.

Grandma sat up and looked at Rose with big wide, innocent eyes. Then she fell backward laughing. "Oh, you should see your face."

"Why would you let me think…."

"That I was having an affair with Jack? That he was an escort?"

Rose nodded her head vigorously.

Grandma shrugged. "Because I'm a bored old lady and it seemed like a hilarious prank to pull on my granddaughter who hasn't had fun in a long, long time. Remember when you convinced me you were joining a Hungarian circus with your boyfriend? I was mad at first, but then I laughed my behind off for weeks. You need a little fun, Rose. I'm worried."

Her heart fell. She had good reason for not having fun. *If I hadn't had so much fun, maybe Mom would still be alive.*

Grandma continued snickering as she lay on the floor.

Ready to kick something, Rose put her hands on her hips instead. "Do you know how worried I've been about you and … him?"

"Oh darling, don't be mad at me. You can't be mad at me. I'm the only relative you've got. And we are going to laugh about this when I get old some day. Really, it was almost as fun as really having a younger male companion." She winked at Jack. "I'll call you when I'm ready for that."

"Honestly, Kate, I don't think I could keep up with you."

Rose turned her glare toward Jack. "And you played right along with this! Making me think…." Rose let out a string of obscenities. All the words she'd been holding back for two years. *Sweet berry muffins my ass.*

When she finally finished, Jack said, "You thought what you wanted to think. I just didn't correct you. I do specialize in older women—as a fitness trainer for senior clients. Ever since my Great Aunt Tildy broke her hip and died, I've tried to get more seniors to work out, build up their bone mass, keep their heart healthy. Although, I didn't believe your grandmother was a senior until I insisted she show me her ID." He winked at her.

"But Grandma, you said you really needed it and that he had a really big…"

"What did you think I meant?"

Her lips wobbled. "A really big p… p…"

"Pectoral muscle?" Jack offered.

Rose figured her face was as red as her beet muffins.

Grandma laughed. "A really big heart, darling. He volunteers as a trainer for seniors at the YMCA. I've hired him as a private instructor. Some of those women down there are so annoying, popping out their false teeth, complaining about their aching joints while they're working out. He's been improving my health, darling. You should be pleased."

"Oh, I am. As punch. It's all good. Great. You're not taking advantage of my grandmother." She flung her arms wide, sending a muffin flying from her basket.

"Oh, he takes advantage of me, alright. He tries to squeeze a few extra crunches out of me every visit."

"Sounds like she's lucky to have you, Jack." I spit out his name.

"Actually, I was thinking he'd be lucky to have you. You'd make a lovely couple," Grandma said.

"Absolutely not."

Jack was shaking his head, too. "Rose doesn't like to have fun. And I most definitely do."

She jerked back. "I do too like to have fun. Just because I'm not a fan of fattening cupcakes and inappropriate juvenile pranks doesn't mean I don't like fun. I like to …" Organize her spices? Return errant shopping carts to their corrals? Rose's heart wasn't slowing down any. "I'm leaving. Enjoy your banana buns."

"Oh, that's not my nickname for Jack. It's granite thighs."

"And there you go with more jokes! I've been worried sick about you, when I should be worried about my bakery, which will probably be closing any day. I haven't been able to concentrate on sales or new recipes…" She paused to take a breath. "And you've been cooking up ways to make me look like a fool!"

Grandma looked horrified and popped up from the floor. "Darling, I had no idea. I'll lend you money."

"No you won't. This is my mess, I'll handle it." Her cheeks still burned from embarrassment. "Get back to your crunches, Grandma. I'm going home to take another look at my budget books from the bakery."

***

Grandma was at knocking on the door of Yum Yum Good For You before Rose even opened the doors for business. "I want six dozen of your best sellers, Rose," she announced, breezing inside with a waft of Chanel in her wake.

"Grandma, you don't have to. You'll never finish six dozen muffins."

"True, but my neighbors will. I'm passing out samples today."

Her eyes got teary. "Really?"

"You have no idea what an astute businesswoman I am Rose. I'm more than just a hot body, you know."

Rose packed up six boxes filled with goodies. "Good luck, Grandma and thanks."

Grandma took the boxes and then paused. "Rose, I'm sorry. I never meant to make you look like a fool. I was just having fun."

Rose nodded, but the embarrassment still stung. She still felt so silly.

After whipping up a few more batches to replenish her stock, Rose wondered if she could keep up. By noon, fourteen of Jack's clients had dropped in, nearly wiping out her stock. As usual, she was working by herself and she panicked, wondering how she was going to wait on customers and make new supplies.

The answer showed up in a dark leather jacket and a wicked grin. "And how's business looking today, Red?"

She crossed her arms and offered her first smile for him. "If business was like this everyday, I'd be making a profit."

"Excellent."

She brushed a coating of flour off her apron. "A little too excellent, I'm almost out of stock."

"Put me to work."

She gave him a doubtful look.

"What? If you need a reference, you can always call your grandmother. I'm a hard worker. I'm sure she's told you so."

"Oh, yes. She's crazy about you." She sighed. "If you're willing I could use the help. Come back to the kitchen."

Rose mixed up batter for carrot raisin muffins and

apple bread, and directed Jack on how to fill the muffin cups while she dashed out to man the register. She sold another three loaves of passion bread, took the muffins from Jack and slid them into the oven, then answered the phone.

When she finally hung up she stared at Jack. "That was the YMCA. They want me to start making them five-dozen kid friendly muffins for their preschool program. Every day." Rose did the mental math. "That's an extra thousand dollars a week."

Jack crossed his arms, quite satisfied. "Fantastic. But is that all?"

She blushed, knowing she owed this all to him. "Ten dozen cupcakes for a reception this weekend. Where did they get the idea I make cupcakes?"

"When I gave them your card, they just assumed a bakery had sweet treats as well. What would be the harm in offering some ooey-gooey desserts? "

"Hey, that's why your clients have to come to you in the first place."

"Good. It'll keep me in business." He winked at her. "Hey, everything's fine in moderation. Why don't you let yourself have any fun at all?"

She started measuring out ingredients for another batch of passion bread. "I spent a long time having nothing but fun. And people got hurt."

He raised an eyebrow, like he was waiting for more of the story.

She shook her head no. "I'm different now. There's no time for fun. I've been busy building my business."

He rested his hand on hers as she stirred the batter; she froze. "If your budget ends up in the black this month, will you allow yourself to have a good time? At least for an hour or so?"

She sighed. "What constitutes a good time?"

"A date. With me."

She swallowed back a nervous squeal. "I thought you weren't interested in me."

"I certainly could be," he said, giving her the once over. "Once you lighten up."

Clearly, the man's eaten a piece of the passion bread, she thought to herself.

"I don't need to lighten up," she said, then silently chastised herself. There were two weeks left in the month; she'd need to sell a lot to come out on top for the month. There was very little chance she'd be going on a date with Jack. "Fine. Help me make some cupcakes and we'll go out if I actually make money this month."

He rubbed his hands together. "I'll start planning it now. I'm no slouch in the kitchen. I used to help Great Aunt Tildy bake Christmas cookies."

"Oh, good," she said, more than a little bit nervous.

Rose scrounged through her supply shelves and realized she didn't even have the right ingredients to make adequate cupcakes for an event. "The cupcakes are going to have to wait until I close," she said, emerging from her storeroom.

"Then I'll be back. For now, I'll take some passion bread for my client tonight."

She narrowed her eyes at him. "Why would you need passion bread for your fitness client?"

He looked offended. "She has a gentlemen friend and she's hoping to move things to the next level."

She wrapped up a few slices and placed them in a

bakery bag. "On the house. Thanks for everything."

"Now, how am I going to get a date with you if you're giving away the store?" He laid some money on the counter and walked out the door, like a hunky hurricane that had upturned everything in her life.

***

She was so distracted, she burned two batches of blueberry bread, set off the smoke alarm and decided to call it a day at five. Remembering very little about making cupcakes and cookies and other sweet treats, she did a few google searches for recipes, dashed to the store for ingredients and started experimenting back at her shop.

She was putting the icing on her first batch of cupcakes when Jack showed up at her door.

"Don't have you a client?" she asked, as she let him in.

"Just finished up with her. Alright, boss, put me to work."

"Taste this. Is it any good?"

He reached for the cupcake and his big fingers brushed hers. It was no wonder dozens of his clients had shown up in her shop today; he could get an Eskimo to buy a sno-cone. He took a bite and nodded while considering the treat. "Not bad."

"But not great. I just don't know how to stand out from all the other cupcake makers out there. The healthy ingredients set me apart. But these..." She gestured to the plate of cupcakes. "There's nothing special about these."

"Try one. See what you think."

She shook her head. "I can't."

"One cupcake isn't going to kill you." He picked

74

one up, peeled off the wrapper and held it in front of her mouth. He twisted it back and forth between his thick fingers. "You know you want it," he said, in a thick, taunting voice.

Her eyes widened and her throat felt thick. "This doesn't seem right for a fitness instructor to be doing."

"We can find a way for you to work it off." A dimple grooved his left cheek.

Her knees wobbled a bit at that—she had a thing for one-dimpled men—but she wasn't going to let him intimidate her with his charm. She reached for the cupcake, but he wouldn't let her take it.

Twisting her lips, she sized up how to take a bite without grazing his skin with her teeth. "What big fingers you have."

He chuckled. "The better to feed you with."

Closing her eyes, she sunk her teeth into the sweet, creamy frosty, then into the spongy, moist cake. Her eyes opened in surprise; it was good. Very good.

Her reaction didn't go unnoticed. "Not bad, huh?" He brushed a crumb off her cheek with his thumb.

And that was enough to give her goose bumps. *Sweet date bread, I'm in trouble.* She took another bite. "Mmm. I feel naughty eating this." She licked her lips. "It's good. But still, it's not special." She tapped her finger on the counter, thinking. How could she make these stand out? She snapped her fingers. "I'm going to use natural ingredients like beet juice and cabbage leaves for food coloring. Herbs like chamomile and valerian for their healing properties."

Rolling his eyes, Jack made a time-out sign with his hands. "Red, they're special for what they are. I promise you, nobody is going to want a cabbage cupcake."

She slumped on a stool in front of her counter.

"Just put some of these out tomorrow and see what happens? And Red? Change your name."

"Fine, I'll admit, it's growing on me when you say it, but I'm not changing my name to Red."

He rolled his eyes. "Your shop's name, not yours. No one else gets to call you Red but me. But Yum Yum Good For You?" He wrinkled his nose. "Sometimes people want to be good. But usually, they don't."

"Oh yeah? And what about you? With a body like that, you look like you're good more often than not."

His laugh sounded like a low, rumbling growl. "I have my bad moments, believe me."

She gulped. Bad boys had been her downfall back in the day. "Not too bad, I hope?"

He grinned at her. "I'll let you find out for yourself."

She backed away from him, like he might devour her just like she'd done to the cupcake. The idea made her shiver. "First I have to make a profit this month."

He took a step closer, so close he could have kissed her. "You will. Call me when those cupcakes sell out tomorrow." Then he backed away and left, flashing a smile on his way out the door.

***

Gluten-free bran bread, he'd been right. She'd sold out of cupcakes before noon. She didn't have to wait to call Jack; he showed up after lunch.

"Congratulations! So, sushi or Italian for our first date?"

She ignored him. "How am I going to serve cupcakes along seaweed muffins?"

"Like I said, everyone's a little naughty and a little nice sometimes. I think people will like the diversity."

***

She delivered the cupcakes to an appreciative audience Friday night.

"The kids have loved your muffins for morning snack. And we love the nutritional value," said the YMCA director. "But these are good too," she said, holding up a cupcake. "Really good."

Rose grabbed a cab to stop at Grandma's. She'd been so busy, she hadn't stopped there in a while—now that she knew Grandma wasn't prey. For the first time, she was hopeful the bakery might be able to stay open a while longer. If the YMCA director liked her muffins and her cupcakes, maybe other customers would accept her mixed offerings, too. But Jack had been right. She couldn't attract cupcake lovers with a name like Yum Yum Good For You.

Grandma gave her a big hug when she walked in. "So, Jack says he's been helping you in the bakery. He's such a nice guy. Really. I know we had some fun at your expense, but give him a chance."

"I don't think I'm his type. I'm vanilla and he wants pina colada."

"You weren't always vanilla, dear. You used to be cayenne pepper." Grandma reached for Rose's hand. "I know your mother's death still weighs heavy on your heart. There's not a day that goes by that I don't think of her. But you've got to move on with your life. What good is it doing depriving yourself of fun?"

"If I hadn't been so wild, Mom would probably still be alive." Her voice came out in a whisper.

Grandma set her other hand on Rose's shoulder.

"Whatever do you mean?"

"I stressed her out. The partying, the slacker boyfriends. She started smoking again when I dropped out of college. She drank more. She put on weight. And then she died. None of that would have happened if I hadn't been *having fun*." She made quote marks in the air. "She told me that all the time. 'You'll be the death of me, Rose.' I was making her sick." Rose closed her eyes and sighed, the tears seeping out of the corners of her eyes. "I owe her something now. I have to be good for her."

Grandma narrowed her brows. "Now you stop right there. She never should have said that to you. Your mother made those decisions, not you. You didn't make her do anything. She had high cholesterol, high blood pressure, and did nothing to fix it! She didn't take her medication like she was supposed to. And you know, she caused me a fair amount of grief when she was younger, but I didn't start smoking and drinking to cope with it."

"She did?"

Grandma nodded. "She started running with the wrong crowd. Her grades dropped. She got suspended for smoking in school. She dropped out senior year. I packed up her clothes for her and told her to get out, get a job, or get back to school."

Rose was stunned. She dropped into a chair. "What happened?"

"She went back to school in a week. Living with her best friend's cousin in a trailer didn't work out so well."

Rose blinked and said nothing for a while. "She never told me that."

"That might explain why she reacted like she did to your rebellious time. I told her it would all work out."

Grandma sighed. "Your mother was unhappy, Rose. Once your father left, she was never the same. You were only two years old, so you don't remember her before that."

Rose nodded. She knew the pain her mother still felt all those years later. Well, Rose had felt it, too, not having a father around.

"Start living your life again. I thought my little prank might remind you how to have fun again, kiddo. I didn't mean to send you into a funk." Grandma's eyes were moist with tears.

"It's okay, Grandma." She rubbed her back. "I was just worried. I can't let anything happen to you."

"I'd be lucky if something like Jack happened to me. And so would you."

Rose felt herself blushing. Grandma noticed. "I think it's time for you to stop being so nice. Try naughty for a change."

Grandma's word clicked something in her brain; something Jack had said, too. Rose hugged her Grandma. "You're a genius. Thank you!" She'd be making a call to the company that created her sign first thing in the morning.

***

Jack had been right; there was a way for her to balance both worlds in her bakery—and in her personal life, too. She called him right when she got to the shop. "When you're done working over your ladies, can you come help with some baking? I'm going to have an open house this weekend introducing my bakery's new name."

"Of course, if it'll get me closer to a date with you. What's the new name?"

"You're going to have to wait to find out."

Jack stopped by first thing in the morning, pestering her the entire time, trying to learn the new name. He'd brush his nose along her cheek and whisper, "Go on Red, tell me your secret."

It just about killed her to keep her mouth closed; she wanted to kiss him and spill the beans. But she liked this game. "I'm going to make you wait."

He groaned. "You are, aren't you?"

She stared at him. "It'll be worth it. Let me get things under control here, first."

He nodded. "Fine. Back to business, slave driver." His grin had her leaning against the wall for support.

Jack distributed fliers to his clients, who promised to pass them out in their apartment buildings, and the director of the Y set fliers out on their reception desk. Rose posted it on Facebook and tweeted it so many times she felt like a chickadee. The sign installer had covered the new sign with a tarp, which could be released by yanking a beautiful gold cord at the open house.

Jack arrived the Saturday morning of the open house in a dark suit and silver tie. Rose reminded herself to breathe. "You clean up nicely, Wolff."

Her took her hand and spun her around, twirling her dress. "And I like you out from under that cape."

The day was unusually warm for February, with a sunny, blue sky. *A good sign*, Rose thought. She hoped her mother was watching. *Please be proud, Mom.*

"So, I've been trying to guess the new name. Is it, "Red's Place?"

"Not even close."

"Jack's Girls?"

She whacked his arm. "You'll find out in fifteen minutes."

Dozens of people showed up for the open house, some having to stand out on the street, waiting for their turn to get in. She heard people complimenting her cupcakes, and two ladies were gushing over the passion bread. A few older women in the corner were having their way with her Sea Goddess Muffins, while proudly feeling each other's biceps.

Everyone followed her outside as she prepared for the unveiling. It had cost some big bucks, but Grandma had told her someone in the building who loved the muffins wanted to be a silent partner and ponied up twenty-five thousand dollars to keep things running. Grandma was handling the details. Rose knew this was the right move that would save her shop. Smiling, she looked at Jack and thought, *"And my heart."*

She stepped in front of the crowd and called for their attention. "Thank you so much for coming out today. I'm excited to announce a new mission for the former Yum Yum Good for You Bakery. A new friend made me realize that you can't always be good. You do need to indulge once in a while. So I'm going to offer you the healthy treats so many of you have come to love, and some decadent desserts as well." She tugged on the golden cord and announced, "At the new Naughty And Nice bakery."

The crowd cheered, and Jack wrapped his arm around her waist and kissed her cheek. "I love it! I hope that's the new plan for you, too."

She raised an eyebrow. "I've decided I need an attitude adjustment, too."

"Well let's get inside and sell some cupcakes so I can start making plans to help you out with that."

Jack was a good salesman, directing his clients to

new goodies, and charming the rest of her customers.
When they finally closed up shop at seven, they slumped
in a pair of bistro chairs at a table covered in crumbs.

Rose swept them away. "That was unbelievable. I
can't thank you enough! I've got several new standing
orders, three events to provide desserts for—and one of
them the healthy options!" She reached across and
squeezed his hands. "You were such a big help."

"Hey, it was good for me, too. I picked up five new
clients."

"I'll probably make a profit this month for sure."

He stood up and her heart dropped. She wasn't
ready for him to leave. "Are you going?"

"Yeah. I'm going to add up your receipts and see
how much you sold today."

She followed him to the register and read out the
totals on each order, while he punched the number into
the calculator on his phone. "Two thousand, three
hundred fifty six dollars and eighteen cents."

Her jaw dropped. "I had no idea."

"And that puts you in the black, doesn't it, Red?"

She nodded. "Alright, when you make reservations
keep in mind I love Italian."

He laughed. "I don't think I can wait that long." He
stood up and held out his hand. "I'm collecting on that
date tonight."

She laughed. "I don't think I could manage it."

"I was thinking of a quiet evening, in."

She raised an eyebrow. "Like with your senior fan
club? I'm not doing lunges."

He smirked that same smirk she'd first seen at
Grandma's a few weeks back. "I'm working on getting
my therapeutic massage license. I could use the practice."

Naughty and Nice. She'd been nice long enough. "Why Jack, you are a wolf, aren't you?" She flicked off the lights and followed him out into the night, her red cape billowing in the breeze.

"I'll let you find out for yourself." His big hands wrapped around her head and he pulled her in for a kiss that was naughty, but also very, very nice.

"Belle"
by Lisa Scott

Belle Foster stood in front of Prince Maxim's apartment in Grimm Towers with her two suitcases at her feet and a whirl of butterflies in her tummy. She rang the bell one more time. *Breathe, breathe, breathe.* Her father had warned her the prince did not run a typical household, but since Dad had suffered his stroke she hadn't been able to press him for further details. He couldn't talk, much less finish his work for the prince. She was determined to save her father's job—because he would recover. He had to.

Tapping her foot impatiently, she rapped on the door. Perhaps the buzzer was broken. Or maybe he was keeping his new carpenter waiting to make a point—he was in charge, and business would be conducted on his time. As she stood in front of the door, a woman in a red cape walked down the hall and approached her.

"Are you here to see the prince?" she asked, surprised.

Belle nodded. "I'm remodeling his library. It's my first day." When she'd approached the prince's assistant about taking over her father's job, he'd offered her room and board while she finished the work so she didn't have to drive in to the city each day.

"Good luck." The woman in red held a white pastry box. "I haven't met him, but I can see his effect on his staff when I make my deliveries."

Belle gulped, just as the door finally opened. A dour man with a balding head and a faded butler's uniform looked at her and then at the woman in the cape. He addressed her first. "The usual, I presume?"

"Of course, six freshly-baked Sea Goddess muffins." She handed the box to him, which he opened, inspecting the goods.

"Very well. You'll charge that to our account and leave yourself a twenty percent gratuity."

"Thank you." She looked as if she might curtsy as she slowly backed away.

The man turned to Belle. "And you're the carpenter?" His eyes flicked over her like he'd discovered an insect he needed to exterminate.

She stuck her chin out. "I am. I'm Leo Foster's daughter. I'm going to finish the library job while my father recovers from his stroke."

"Very well. Follow me." Leading her inside, he held the box out in front of him as if it might detonate. "Seaweed muffins," he explained with a shudder. "The prince has a standing order every other day. Makes no sense to me why you'd eat a muffin made with the garbage they dredge off beaches, but rule number one— never question the prince."

She nodded at that bit of advice. Her father had told her something similar when he'd first started working here.

They walked down the marble entryway that led into a huge, high-ceilinged living room. She tried to stifle a whistle, and was so busy gawking at the paneled walls and exquisite crown molding, that she didn't notice the line of staff members waiting to meet her. "Oh, hey," she said when she noticed them inspecting her with the same curiosity she had for her new surroundings. She bit her lip. "I mean, hello." She'd been trying to improve her vocabulary before starting here, but she doubted she'd ever sound suitable for a royal—or his staff.

The butler cleared his throat. "Ms. Foster, I am Reginald Parks, the prince's butler and house manager. I'd like to introduce you to Mrs. Downing, our housekeeper."

A cheery, plump woman nodded at Belle. "You'll fit in just fine, deary."

Next he introduced Courtney Wilson, the chef. She was thirty-something with short, dark hair, and an eyebrow ring. She grinned. "Company. This is a first. I can't wait to cook for someone besides the prince."

Reginald hissed at her. "Watch your place, Courtney."

Her smile fell and she bowed her head.

"No visitors ever?" Belle asked

"Never," Courtney said quietly, looking up. "Not in the six years I've been here."

"Not even a girlfriend?"

"What girlfriend?" Courtney asked with a snort.

Mrs. Downing drew in a breath. "Hush, child. He might hear you."

"The prince does not have company in any shape or form. And there will be no more discussion about that." Reginald frowned, but continued. "Next, is the prince's assistant, Nicholas Ridgeway."

A tall, thin man in wire-rimmed glasses looked up from his phone. "If you need to ask anything of the prince, you come to me. You will not have any contact with him."

That was a surprise. "What if I have a question about the project? Or if I need to ask his opinion?"

Nicholas raised an eyebrow. "Then you'll be asking me."

Belle pursed her lips and nodded. Her father hadn't been exaggerating.

"Nicholas will drive you to visit your father three times a week, unless of course there is an emergency. Please give him a schedule of your planned visits. And finally," Reginald continued, "This is Rory Kirkpatrick, the prince's dog keeper."

A wiry young man smiled and waved. "He's got three Irish wolfhounds. I'll do my best to keep them out of your way." As if on cue, they came tearing down the hall, practically knocking Belle down.

"Off you beasts, off!" Rory said in a thick, Irish brogue. The dogs looked disappointed, and slunk off to the corner, where they collapsed on velvet doggie beds.

Belle let out the breath she'd been holding. "Very nice to meet you all."

"Let me show you to your room, dear, so you can get settled in," said Mrs. Downing. "Reginald, carry the poor girl's bags." Reginald looked put out, but he did as he was told. He might think he was in charge of the household, but Belle was starting to see the pecking order already; and Reginald wasn't at the top.

Belle followed them past the grand staircase that led to the second floor of the penthouse. "The prince's living quarters," Mrs. Downing explained to Belle. They passed the kitchen, a solarium, and the library where Belle would be working.

"It's an enormous apartment," Belle said.

"Yes. His penthouse takes up half the top two floors," Mrs. Downing said with pride.

Then they passed a closed room that gave off a dark, sad feeling. "What's that?" she asked.

Mrs. Downing sighed. "It was the ballroom. The

prince used to throw magnificent parties there. It fits two-hundred people, you know." She shrugged. "Now it's just used for storage."

Reginald scowled at Mrs. Downing. "This way, Ms. Foster." He led her down another hall and opened a door at the end.

"Servants' wing," Mrs. Downing said. "I'm one room over from you."

"She snores," Reginald said.

"I beg your pardon," Mrs. Downing said through clenched teeth. "You should be so lucky as to know anything about my sleeping habits." Her cheeks were flushed and she busied herself picking at something on the skirt of her tight uniform.

"You have your own private bathroom," Reginald said, ignoring Mrs. Downing. "We take breakfast at seven, lunch at noon, and dinner is served promptly at six-thirty."

"Will the prince be having dinner with us?"

"No," Mrs. Downing said with a sigh. "He takes his meals in his room."

"Why is he such a loner?" Belle asked.

Mrs. Downing and Reginald looked at each other but said nothing.

Realizing she wouldn't be getting an answer to that question, Belle shrugged.

Reginald cleared his throat. "I'll send Nicholas for you in half an hour to show you the library where you'll be working."

"Good. Once I get a look at where my father left off, I can tell you how long the job'll take to finish."

They left her in her room, and she unpacked her clothes and toiletries, marveling at the splendor of even the servant's quarters. She still lived at home with her father outside the city, while she established her custom furniture business. Their small, two-bedroom ranch could've fit inside the living room and front hall of the prince's apartment. Too bad she'd never meet the man during her stay. Would've been nice to say she'd known a prince.

***

Prince Maxim crouched in the shadows at the top of the stairs, hoping to hear the woman's voice again. He'd caught just a glimpse of her slim figure, and her long, chestnut hair as she passed. But her sweet, melodic voice had intrigued him. How he'd enjoyed hearing her say his name, watching her lips and tongue move over each word in his title: Prince Maxim Phillip Alexander Whitney Duquesne the third.

He could certainly go downstairs and introduce himself and then take her hands in his. Would the fingers of a woman carpenter be rough or soft? He could find out with the shake of a hand, with a kiss to her palm. Women had fainted before just from that gesture of his. It was so much more unexpected than a kiss to the back of the hand. It had become his trademark move for the women who'd most intrigued him.

Back in his country, the press had dubbed him Prince Swoon. Women waited outside the castle for a glimpse of him. Truthfully, he hadn't been kind to many of them. They were pretty playthings, and the line of willing women stretched miles long. For Maxim hadn't just been a prince, but a handsome prince. The thing of fairy tales, the press liked to remind its readers.

How things change, he thought, sitting there in the shadows. Now, he couldn't even tolerate to glance at himself in the mirror. He'd taken care of that problem by painting them all black. Even Nicholas couldn't look him in the face. Maxim was a freak now, and he'd never be able to return home. Even cloistered here in his apartment, he was powerless to approach just one woman downstairs, let alone face millions of his loyal subjects again. They knew he was a disfigured recluse living in America. He wouldn't subject himself to their horrified looks and pity. Belle was sure to have the same reaction when she saw his scars. He swore to himself. In the end, his ex-girlfriend had taken away so much more than his looks; she'd cursed him to be alone for the rest of his life. Vivian had told him he didn't know how to love. She'd been right. But now, he'd never have the chance to learn.

He stalked back to his chambers and kicked his desk chair out of the way. It toppled over onto the floor. The balcony doors beckoned, covered in heavy, damask drapes. Occasionally, on moonlit nights, he'd stand out there and look over the city, enjoying the cool breeze on his skin. He never dared go out in the daytime; night was the only safe time for him. But usually the memory of Vivian and what happened on that horrible night out there on the balcony chased him back inside.

With one finger, he parted the curtains ever so slightly, the sunlight stinging his eyes. He closed the tiny gap and crossed the room, sitting on his bed. He hadn't felt torment like this in a long time. *Belle.* Then again, there hadn't been a woman in his apartment save for the servants since the disaster with Vivian.

No, he wouldn't be meeting this woman. Only dreaming of her. He lay back on his bed and stared at the ceiling. His dark room soothed him. It was here he conducted his business, handling his investments and the occasional correspondence required as a member of the royal family. From here, he still could make his mark on the world—without ever having to be part of it. His title was only ceremonial; there was no one back home he was letting down in his absence. Except of course his parents, who had begged him not to go to America when he'd met the beautiful woman who'd upended his life.

He ran his fingers across the rough edges of the skin on his cheek, over his nose and down to his mouth. The pain she'd caused was etched in his brain and on his face. His mother had warned him that Vivian was 'not the right kind of girl' for him. But what warm-blooded male would've thought 'run' after finding a swimsuit model clad only in a fur coating waiting for him in his backyard?

If only he had run. He certainly wouldn't have moved to America with her. And he wouldn't be the shell of a man he was now, living in the dark, dreaming of what had been. He could never go back to his country now. Never. He'd live out his days waiting for moments of surprise. *Like the one downstairs right now.*

He needed to know more about Belle. He logged onto the Internet and searched for what information he could find about the daughter of Leo Foster. He wanted a picture to put to her voice; fact to fill in the fantasy he'd weave. But nothing turned up. He called Nicholas. "Get me all the information you have on the girl."

"I already have."

The prince paused, trying to keep anger from creeping into his voice. "Then bring it to me."

"I've been waiting for you to ask."

"And I want to see her appropriately dressed for dinner."

"You'll be joining us?" Nicholas asked, surprised.

"Of course not. But I do want to see her."

Nicholas nodded and left the room.

***

Nicholas led Belle to the library, where she'd be working. The sight of her father's tools made her gasp. "Oh, Dad," she whispered.

Nicholas heard her. "Your father did good work. We hope you can continue with the project in the same quality fashion."

"Of course I can. He taught me everything I know." She ran her fingers across the ornate bookshelves he'd been building. "I'm a furniture designer, but I can totally continue the finishing work my father started." She grinned at him. "Detail work is my specialty."

"Good. Then I'll let you get to it. I'll send someone for you when lunch is ready."

"Can you just bring it to me? I don't want to stop working." She wanted to finish this job as quickly as she could. She'd only been here for an hour, but the quiet rooms, the closed doors, and the overall somber feeling were getting to her already.

"Very well. But I'm certain the staff will insist you join us for dinner at six-thirty. Which means you'll want to stop work at six to freshen up first."

"Okay. Sounds good." Belle waited until he left before she grabbed her father's hammer. Feeling foolish, she reached for his tool belt and held it against her chest, feeling him there with her. But then she pushed aside her sentimentality and got to work. "The sooner I finish this, the sooner I can get back to you," she whispered.

The beautiful mahogany finials and trim she needed to complete the shelves were neatly stacked in the corner of the room. She spotted a sketch for the complex crown molding he was planning to install, and realized the job was going to be a bit more involved than she'd thought.

Two or three weeks, depending on how things unfolded. In an old building like this, there were bound to be a few surprises that popped up. Every project had its delays. A month tops, that's what she'd tell Nicholas. Then she'd get back to her father and hopefully he'd be ready for rehabilitation. The nurses had her number and were to call her if his condition changed. She knew what she was doing here was for the best.

She started trimming the bookcases, enjoying the smell of the wood, the warmth of the sunlight streaming through the window, and the thrill that came with a new project. The morning flew by, and she paused briefly to devour a delicious Caesar salad for lunch. She was proud of her work, and hoped her father would be, too. There'd be no pleasing her ex-boyfriend, Stewart. He'd been impatient for her to lose her interest in her silly furniture-making hobby. When she rented space to work on her custom furniture, he realized she was serious and left her. A woman who worked with her hands wasn't the right prop for a guy hoping to make partner in a law firm he wasn't even working in yet.

But still, Stewart had had goals and dreams and plans while he toiled away in law school, and Belle had realized far too late, hers were much different. Belle wasn't one to waste time, and she'd wasted two good years on Stewart. She frowned. *If a future lawyer disapproved of a female carpenter, what would a sitting prince think?* she wondered.

Apparently, it didn't matter, since she wouldn't be meeting him. She finished her salad, got back to work and by the time six o'clock came, she'd completed two bookcases. With twenty more to go—and the crown molding, she'd be a busy woman the next few weeks. Hard work always left her hungrier than she realized, and she was hoping another delicious meal was on its way. That's another thing a prince wouldn't be impressed with—her incredible appetite.

She went back to her room and found three beautiful evening dresses hanging on the door, with a note from Mrs. Downing. "I doubted very much that you'd brought appropriate dinner attire. I took the liberty of purchasing a few things. See you at dinner."

That was another thing she and Stewart had fought about. She hated going to his charity functions, playing dress up and making happy talk with people who were busy scanning the room for someone more important to talk to. A prince would probably be even worse like that.

She took the dresses off the door and sighed. They were beautiful. But why did she need to dress up for dinner with the staff? She showered and changed into a pale blue cocktail dress that skimmed her knees and showed off her toned arms. Her job kept her in good shape, but never before required her to don eveningwear. This was a first. Building bookshelves for Prince Maxim would definitely be remembered as her strangest job ever.

The staff was dressed in formal serving clothes, and stood waiting by the table as she walked into the dining room. She wondered if someone else was going to be joining them. The dining table looked as if it could seat fifty, but it was set for six. Lush flower arrangements lined the length of the table. A huge candelabrum was lit with dozens of glowing tapers.

"This is just for us?"

Courtney rolled her eyes. "We've never had the chance to throw a dinner party here. And Nicholas takes my meals up to the Prince. I don't even get to see the look of pleasure on his face when he tastes my exquisite lamb roast. Just indulge us." She gestured to the table. "Please, be our guest."

Reginald pulled out her chair, and the indulging was all on their end: appetizers, a soup and salad course, a

fresh lemon sorbet to cleanse her palate. At least, that's
what they told her it was for. She'd thought dinner was
finished and they were having sherbet for dessert. That
led to a few strained laughs until Belle almost busted a gut
when she found out with the little lemon scoop was really
for. "The last time anyone washed my mouth out it was
for experimenting with a certain foul word when I was
six, not to make way for more food." They'd laughed so
hard at that, she feared they'd bother the prince.

Belle was full after the fish course, enjoying the
conversation with the staff, while Courtney flitted to and
from the kitchen, stopping to taste her creations and ask
Belle what she thought, before popping back up to bring
out the next course.

Mrs. Downing turned on light classical music, and
more laughter soon filled the air. Even the dogs joined
the party, bounding into the room, rewarded with scraps
from the table.

Then Courtney came out with the main course.
"Crab-stuffed filet mignon," she announced.

Belle settled her hands over her stomach. "I
couldn't."

Courtney pointed the serving fork at her. "You
must."

Belle dropped her head back. Was there such a
thing as a food hangover? She was sure to find out the
next day. They'd been eating and talking for hours.

"You're such an amazing cook. And you threw
together such a beautiful dinner party. Why are you guys
working here, when you can only share your talents with a
client you never even see?"

Courtney set down the serving platter and dished
out the meat. Her smile disappeared. "I want to open my
own restaurant some day. The Prince pays me double
what I'd make anywhere else right now, plus free room
and board. I'd be crazy to quit." She didn't sound
entirely convincing.

"I couldn't leave the prince," Mrs. Downing said, setting her hand over her heart. "I've been with him since he moved to America eight years ago."

"Same here," said Rory.

Reginald pursed his lips. "I'll be with the prince until I die."

"Enough, already." Courtney forced a smile. "This is a party. Let's celebrate the arrival of our new guest. Eat up!"

The dogs stared at the table mournfully, hoping for a few more bits of food, while Belle regaled them with a tale about the time she worked with a man who'd cut off two fingers with a circular saw. "And he was still able to…." Her words trailed off as she watched four sets of eyes shift to the hall. She followed their gaze, and saw a figure dash away. "Was that the prince?"

Reginald rose from the table. "Yes. We've upset him." He left the table and hurried out the door.

Mrs. Downing flicked off the music. "He was such a lovely man before…" She stopped herself, as if she'd said too much.

"Before?" Belle asked.

Nervous looks flashed between the four staff members still in the room.

Courtney sighed. "Before his crazy girlfriend killed herself and ruined his life."

Belle gasped.

"Quiet! We are not to speak of it!" Rory said, covering the ears of the dog sitting at his feet.

Courtney shrugged. "He loves my lasagna too much to fire me."

"What did his girlfriend do?" Belle asked quietly.

This time, Mrs. Downing spoke up. "His girlfriend Vivian was … intense. She wanted to get married, so of course, he decided it was time to break up." She sighed, like an old radiator.

"What happened?"

Courtney picked up the story with a hushed voice. "She lured him out to the balcony where she jumped to her death. After throwing acid in his face."

Shaking her head, Belle covered her mouth to keep the scream in her throat.

"She said if he wouldn't love her, she was going to be sure no one would ever love him. And then she jumped." Mrs. Downing's voice cracked.

Belle felt tears in her eyes. "What did the acid do to him?"

"It left him grotesquely disfigured. Or so his doctor said. I've never seen him," Courtney said.

Mrs. Downing pulled a small picture from her apron pocket and handed it to Belle. She took the picture, fingering its frayed corners as she studied it. A dark-haired young man in uniform looked up at her. He appeared grim, as if he'd known what was to come. But he was handsome; undeniably, the most gorgeous man she'd ever seen, with chiseled features, light blue, deep-set eyes and a lock of thick curls that fell over his forehead. Basically, exactly what you'd expect a prince to look like. "He's so handsome." She gazed at him a little longer before handing the picture back to Mrs. Downing.

"He was. He hasn't let any of us see him since. He's stayed in his chambers since he left the hospital six years ago." Mrs. Downing slipped the photo back in her apron and started gathering the dirty plates from the table.

Belle struggled to swallow. Mrs. Downing set her hand on Belle's shoulder. "I'm sorry. We shouldn't have told you. We're not to speak of it, but it's a sadness we all carry with us. And now you do, too."

Belle nodded, disappointed their fun evening was ending on such a sad note. "Can I help you clean up?"

"No, we've got everything covered," Courtney said.

"I'm going to turn in. Thanks for a lovely dinner." Belle trudged to her room and had a hard time sleeping that night, imagining what the rugged face of the prince looked like now.

***

"No more parties!" shouted the prince, slamming his fist on his desk.

Nicholas spread his hands apart. "It wasn't a party. It was dinner with our new guest. She's going to be staying here for a while. We want her to feel comfortable, so she's relaxed to finish her job."

"Even my dogs abandoned me!" The prince ran his hand through his hair. It was getting long, and he was due for another cut. He buzzed it to his scalp every six months; he wouldn't let anyone come in to cut it. Life could be difficult when you spent it locked away. And here he'd thought it would be the simplest solution— hiding. It was surely easier than facing the world again.

"You could always join us, your highness."

The prince laughed, though he wasn't amused. They both knew Nicholas called him your highness when he was trying to sway Max. "You can't even bear to look at me, you think the rest of the staff could? You think Belle wouldn't recoil at the sight of me?" He spat out the words.

Nicholas raised his eyes to him. "I don't look at you, your highness, because I know it makes you uncomfortable when I do. But when I do catch a glimpse of you, I see the same man I've always served."

Maxim turned from him; he *was* uncomfortable with Nicholas' gaze. "That's enough from you tonight, Nicholas." He was feeling calmer, though his heart rate wasn't slowing. He was still thinking about Belle. Maybe he was wrong. Maybe she wouldn't gape in horror at him. Someone with such a pleasant laugh couldn't be cruel, could they?

He'd had all day to look over the research and photos. Belle Foster was training to be a master carpenter, she won a spelling bee when she was twelve, enjoyed reading in her spare time, and she photographed

98

very well. Which made him even angrier to hear her laughing and enjoying herself downstairs while he had lingered at the tops of the stairs eavesdropping like an outcast, imaging he'd been part of the fun.

Nicholas let himself out of the room. The prince sighed. He wasn't angry about the party. He was angry he hadn't been brave enough to be part of it. He was angry Vivian had been right; no woman would ever love him again.

From time to time, Nicholas asked him why he didn't try more reconstructive surgery. He'd undergone three rounds. But doctors had told him they wouldn't be able to totally repair the damage. He'd never be the same, and anything less than what he had been wasn't acceptable.

His three dogs had slunk back to his room, and slumbered at the foot of his bed in a shaft of moonlight that shone through a gap in the curtains. He reached down and scratched Duke behind the ear. His leg twitched in response. He liked the feel of the dogs' wiry fur against his skin. Max hadn't felt the touch of a human in six years, since he'd holed up in this room.

Three Sea Goddess muffins remained in the box. He broke one in half and tossed it to the dog closest to him. King's head popped up and he snatched the muffin midair. When Nicholas had brought up samples from a new bakery, he thought they'd be the perfect treat for his dogs. He wasn't concerned about healthy foods for himself. He ate what he wanted; it was one of the few pleasures left.

His days started with a shower and breakfast in the morning. The next few hours were devoted to reviewing the news from around the world. He broke for lunch and did some reading for enjoyment. Then he attended to whatever business was at hand for the day— reviewing correspondence from his country, checking his investments. He spent a few hours each afternoon lifting weights and running on his treadmill. He was in good shape for a hermit. Dinner followed his workout, and then he faced the long, long evenings. The nights were the worst. Once upon a time, it had been his favorite time of day, filled with drinks and dancing and beautiful women.

That's probably why he'd been so upset with the dinner party one floor below. Now he was embarrassed by his behavior. Surely, Belle had heard him blustering about when he ran from the stairs. How could he make it up to her? Let her know the recluse prince wasn't totally lacking in manners in refinement?

He tossed another hunk of muffin to Duke, and Queenie was soon looking for a treat too, so he gave her the rest. He spent the rest of the night mulling over what he could give Belle as an apology. How could he show her he wasn't the beast he surely seemed to be? And he couldn't stop thinking about what Nicholas had said: you could always join us.

But he truly couldn't, could he?

***

Belle jumped every time she heard an unfamiliar noise the next day as she worked on the bookcases. She dropped a handful of nails when Mrs. Downing rapped on the door to ask if she'd like some tea. She was expecting the prince—or his assistant—to come down and fire her for causing a ruckus in his home last night.

Kneeling on the ground, she searched for the tiny nails scattered on the hardwood floor. She couldn't stop thinking about the handsome prince in that picture and his piercing eyes. The poor man, feeling like such an outcast that he hid away in this gorgeous apartment. Would he even use this library she was finishing?

It was no matter. Her father would be paid, and hopefully get future work from the prince. Picking up the last nail, she sat back on her heels and sighed. It was going to be a long month working here with the mysterious man lurking above, watching and listening in the shadows.

Her head snapped up when she heard a creak in the hall. Nicholas rapped on the door. "May I disturb you for a moment?"

She stood up "Certainly."

He walked in with an enormous vase of bright flowers. She spotted roses in the bunch, and others far too fancy for her to know.

"These are from the prince. He'd like to apologize for his outburst last night."

Belle stuffed the nails in the pouch of her tool belt. "This wasn't necessary." She took the flowers from him, her cheeks burning.

"He wasn't himself last night. He's a very dignified, distinguished man. He's afraid he gave you the wrong impression."

She smoothed her hands down her thighs. "I'm sorry we disturbed him."

"Don't think twice about it. Can I tell him his apology is accepted?"

"Of course. And can you tell him he's more than welcome to come and see the work in progress to be sure its to his liking?"

Nicholas forced a smile. "I'll tell him. But he won't come."

"If he never leaves his chambers, why did he have this library made?"

Nicholas shrugged. "He uses an ereader, but he wants a home for his books. He has many first editions, you know. I've told him you're continuing your father's quality work. How is he?"

"I call the hospital three times a day. No change in his condition. I'm hoping to see him soon." She frowned. She couldn't stop to think about her father, or she'd collapse in tears and be no good for the rest of the day. She had to plow through this job so she could get back to his side.

Nicholas pursed his lips. "I'll leave you to your work."

***

After lunch, she paused to admire her flowers. She'd never gotten such a gorgeous bouquet. When Stewart did think to send flowers—usually after a fight he hadn't been able to win—he'd send the obligatory dozen red roses, without a card. None of those bouquets had brought her close to the same thrill as the one sitting in front of her. And she had no idea why.

She picked up her hammer, ready to start the next bookshelf, when she heard another creak in the hall. "You know, I could look into fixing the squeaky floorboard if you'd like, Nicholas."

There was no answer, just an intake of breath. Goosebumps spread up her arms. The prince was in the hall watching her; she knew it. But more than startled, she was worried her reaction would frighten him away. "Would you like to come in and look at my work, Prince Maxim? You're going to have a beautiful library, soon. I pride myself in flawless work."

She waited to hear the rustle of clothing as he rushed away, the quick movement of departing feet, but it was silent. She dared not move; neither did he.

Then a low, deep voice said, "Flawless is good. Something I'm no longer used to in my life."

She regretted her words immediately. She didn't know what to say. Luckily, he continued. "But I didn't come to check on your work. I came to see if you liked the flowers. Nicholas said you were pleased, but he would say that. I had to see for myself."

She had her back to him and didn't turn to look; that would spook him away for sure. "They are truly the most lovely flowers I've ever received. Not that I've gotten many."

"I find that hard to believe." He was quiet for another moment, and she hoped to hear his footsteps headed her way, but no such luck.

Well, he'd taken a chance coming down here; now so would she. "You have a wonderful, talented staff. The only thing missing from dinner last night was you. I'd be so pleased if you'd join us tonight."

He didn't answer right away. That was a good sign. "I will have Nicholas let you know. I usually take meals alone."

"I certainly hope you consider it. I'd love to get to know you."

"I must warn you, if you like things flawless, you will be disappointed."

She cursed to herself. "I like flawless work. Human beings are flawed by nature. I find new flaws in myself every day. Why just last night I made a prince feel uncomfortable in his own home."

"And I made my guest feel unwelcome. We're even." Another pause. "I will join you for dinner, Miss Foster. But on my terms. I'm not as comfortable with my flaws yet as you are with yours. And you have none from where I'm standing."

Thank god her back was to him so he couldn't see her blush. "Whatever your conditions are, I'm fine with them. And I look forward to dinner."

"As do I." She could hear the grin in his voice, then quiet footsteps headed toward the staircase.

***

Clothes were strewn about the room, and another shirt went flying onto the bed. It didn't matter what he'd be wearing. She'd be able to see nothing but the scars on his skin, the shame on his face. Would she pretend they weren't there? Should he tell her right from the start what had happened to him? Address the elephant in the room the moment she arrived?

He'd been ridiculous agreeing to this. He was more nervous than the time he was first presented to the public as a full-fledged, adult prince. But he hadn't wanted anything this badly since ... well, he couldn't remember. Since he was a child and longed for a suit of armor and a white horse on Christmas so he could be a proper prince? He took another look at the picture of Belle that Nicholas

103

had printed from the internet, and that gave him the resolve to step into the first tux he'd tried on, slip into his cloak and shoes and head for the dining room.

***

Belle checked herself in the mirror one last time before she left for the dining room. She'd chosen the pale pink dress Mrs. Downing had bought her. She'd styled her hair in an updo, then changed her mind and brushed it out so it fell around her shoulders. Then she'd pulled it back; then took it down. She hadn't brought much makeup, so she had to settle for the one shade of lipstick she'd brought.

As she entered the dining room, she realized it wouldn't matter. The room was dark, save for two candles lit in the middle of the table. There were two place settings—one at the very end, and another three seats down. Three flower arrangements that looked like they belonged in a hotel lobby lined the table. Soft, classical music played from somewhere in the room. The aroma of a savory roast set her mouth watering.

Nicholas walked in and pulled her chair out for her. "Please have a seat. The prince will be right down. The rest of the staff has been given the evening off. I'll be serving you tonight."

Her eyes widened.

"Don't worry. Courtney prepared the meal, but the prince … he wanted me to handle this most special occasion." Nicholas lowered his voice. "Truly, we've seen nothing like this since his incident."

Belle nodded, and her fingers shook as she spread the napkin on her lap, so she sat on her hands for a moment hoping to still them. Deciding a drink might help, she took a long sip of the wine already poured for her, wishing it'd been a shot of whiskey instead. The minutes ticked by. She finished the wine and wondered if she was being stood up.

And then the energy in the room changed. She didn't hear him, but she knew he was there. She looked up, and he stood silhouetted in the entryway to the room.

"I apologize for my lateness, I was detained." He sighed. "Actually, I was nervous."

"Me, too. I'm just glad you came. It smells delicious and I've been dying to eat Courtney's food. She's incredible."

She heard him laugh and felt embarrassed to have gushed over the meal. They weren't here for the meal. "I was looking forward to seeing you as well." She cursed herself for choosing the word 'see.' She sighed. The prince was sure to regret their dinner before the night was over. "I didn't mean that I wanted to see...."

"You're uncomfortable. I'm sorry." He walked closer, but not too close, and strapped his arms across his chest. "Let's just get this out of the way. My face was severely disfigured in an accident with a woman I didn't treat well. As such, I can't stand to see myself nor for others to see me."

"Now wait a minute," Belle said, annoyed. "It wasn't an accident, she threw acid in your face. And it doesn't matter whether you treated her well or not, no one deserves what she did to you."

He said nothing.

"I can google you just as easy as you can google me." So that was a bit of a lie, but she didn't want to get the staff in trouble.

"Fair enough."

"And you did say we should get this out in the open."

He chuckled. "Indeed, I did. You're bolder than your internet search indicated."

"Trust me, Prince Maxim, I didn't come to gawk at you. I came to meet the man who has a collection of antique inkwells from the desk of the most famous people in history. Who rescues Irish Wolf Hounds. And who builds an elaborate library he'll never set foot in just so his books have a place to call home."

"Precious things deserve beautiful surroundings. That's why I insisted on decorating the dining room tonight. For you."

Her blush must've been visible even in the dark room.

He walked past her to his seat at the end of the table. He wore a hooded cloak that hung well over his forehead. She doubted she'd be able to see his face even with all the lights on in the room. But if the candlelight made him more comfortable, she was glad.

"I wasn't sure what you liked, so I asked Courtney to make a few different entrees."

"As long as it's not sushi, we're good." She hoped she sounded calmer than she felt.

"How is your father?" He picked up his wine glass, swirling the liquid.

She smoothed her hand across the tablecloth. "The same. But he'll get better. I know it."

The prince nodded. "You're a good worker, just like him. I have to admit, I wasn't expecting the same quality from…." He let the thought hang there, but she knew what he meant.

"From a woman. I know."

"No, I meant from someone so young. It takes a while to achieve the skill you've mastered."

"I'm sorry. I just assumed you meant because I'm a woman." She cleared her throat. "I'm a bit defensive. My ex-boyfriend left me because he was embarrassed by what I do."

"Then your ex was a fool twice over—for leaving you, and for his reasoning. What you do is art."

Her heart swelled. That's what she'd always told her ex. She did consider herself to be an artist. "I've been working at my daddy's knee since I can remember."

"I'm lucky to have you here. And I'm sorry you lost your mother."

It was so long ago, she couldn't even remember her face without looking at a picture. "How did you know?"

He paused for a moment. "I asked Nicholas to tell me everything he knew about you."

"Even the time I got grounded for smuggling a family of baby raccoons in my room when I was ten?"

"He left that part out. Nicholas!" he called. "You're fired." He laughed, a wonderful, confident laugh.

"Then maybe you also know I've been trying my hardest to sound formal and polished, but that just isn't me."

"Just be yourself, Belle. I like you."

"As long as you're being yourself, we've got a deal."

"Good."

Dinner was soon served, and their conversation flowed naturally, but she kept her gaze averted for much of it, hoping she wouldn't lose the easy rapport they'd fallen into. But she couldn't help wondering how the evening would end. Things were fine so long as they were ten feet apart. Would they get any closer than that?

But after dessert was served and their coffees were drained, the prince rose from his seat, and tugged his cloak down over his forehead. "Close your eyes," he commanded.

Of course, she looked at him and blinked instead. "Why?"

He laughed softly. "You're the first woman to question everything I do. It's different. Will you just trust me and close them?"

"Okay." She closed her eyes and heard him walking toward her. Then he lifted her hand, pressed his lips against her palm and said, "Goodnight, my artist."

She shivered. "Are you ever going to feel comfortable letting me see you?"

"I hope so."

***

It went better than he could have hoped for. Belle was funny and kind, challenging and intriguing—qualities he couldn't have gleaned from Nicholas' search. It would've been so much easier if she'd been a doting bore, because he didn't know what to do with this feeling echoing inside him; familiar and strange at the same time.

But having dinner in a darkened dining room was one thing. What was next for them? What could a man—voluntarily confined to his chambers—offer a bright, curious, beautiful woman?

He ran his fingers over his face. Was he remembering his scars to be worse than they really were? The rough edges of the damage felt like an old puzzle he hadn't attempted to put together in a long time. Right after the accident when he was sent home and the searing pain had disappeared, he couldn't keep his hands off his face; touching it again and again to prove to himself this had really happened.

He had to see for himself. He hadn't looked at his own face in two years. Maybe it wasn't so bad. He was building it up in his mind, that was it. The only mirror in his room that wasn't covered in black paint was tucked in a trunk in the back of his closet. Rifling through shoes and clothes and boxes of unopened liquor, he pulled the trunk out and took a deep breath.

He brought the mirror close to his face, so he could only see his eyes. Fortunately, his vision had been spared, although the scarring did pull open his left eye ever so slightly so that half his face looked perpetually surprised. The left side of his face from the cheekbone down had suffered most of the damage. He pulled the mirror slowly away, revealing the smooth, raised scar in a shape almost perfectly circular on his cheek. Then it traveled down to his chin, pulling half his mouth down in a permanent grimace.

No, it wasn't as bad as he remembered; it was worse. He threw the mirror across the room and opened the bottle of scotch sitting on his desk. He'd been a fool thinking Belle could ever be interested in him.

Vivian was probably laughing from above.

Scratch that. She was laughing from the depths of hell.

***

Three days later, Belle couldn't shake the disappointment that the prince hadn't come to see her again while she worked. And she was really hoping he would have arranged another private dinner. Perhaps he'd only been kind, pretending to be interested in their conversation. Perhaps she'd been too bold. Or maybe too boring. She sighed as she sanded a piece of trim.

She hadn't told her father about the prince's behavior during her trips to the hospital. She'd visited her father twice since she'd moved into the prince's apartment. Her father's condition hadn't worsened, but it hadn't improved either.

She was finishing another bookcase when she heard a voice in the hall. "You're making quicker progress than I'd imagined. I hope you're not in a hurry to leave." It was Maxim.

Her heart tightened. "I thought you'd be pleased I'm efficient."

"I'll have to come up with a few more projects for you."

She nailed the piece of trim in place, aware he was watching her every move. "What else do you have in mind?"

"You tell me. What would you do if this were your home?"

She sat back, still without looking in his direction. "If this were my home, I'd want a big workshop to use for my furniture making business. I'd revamp the ballroom and throw wild parties that left all the neighbors gossiping, and I'd be sure the banister was strong enough so I could slide down it each morning instead of taking the stairs." She felt herself blushing and looked down at her hands, still clenching the hammer. "Of course, that's quite a bit different from what you want, I'm sure."

109

"I'm sure you can understand why I'm not one to throw parties."

She sighed. It might cost her her job, but she was just going to come out and say it. "Maxim, you are a funny, kind, generous man. Do you really think I or anyone else would think any differently after seeing the scars on your face?"

He didn't scream or order her out. No, it was worse; he said nothing.

She softened her voice and set down her hammer. "Don't you trust me?"

"Trust is a hard thing to keep after what happened to me, Belle."

"Then she's going to punish you from her grave forever. Maxim, I like you. I'd like to get to know you better. But if you're not willing to take the chance, I understand. I think you and your staff and even this beautiful apartment deserve to hear laughter and joy again."

He said nothing for so long, she figured he'd left. But then he sighed and said, "Would you do me the honor of joining me for dinner again?"

"In candlelight and shadows again?"

"I'll do my best, Belle. I'll leave you to your work now."

***

Belle chose the dress she'd worn the first night she joined the staff for dinner. Surprisingly, no one had questioned her about her dinner with the prince. She headed for the dining room, hoping to find it brighter than last time, but again, only a few candles lit the space. *At least he's coming*, she thought.

She took her seat as before, but didn't have to wait as long for him to arrive this time. "I'm not ready to abandon the security of the darkness yet, Belle. But I may have a surprise or two for you."

"I like surprises."

They chatted about their travels; his thirty-two countries, to her twelve U.S states.

She fingered her glass of wine on the table, turning it round and round by the steam. "What about your country? Is it beautiful?"

He leaned back in his chair, his posture becoming relaxed. "The most beautiful I've seen. It's often been said my country has extraordinarily handsome men, and women who are among the most beautiful in the world. Which is why I could never return. Not like this."

"Your people must miss you."

He ignored her, and changed the topic. "What kind of furniture are you making?"

She told him about the custom made desks she was creating, and the difficulty adding a wet bar into one that a client had ordered.

"Now I know your next project for me. A desk with a mini-fridge and a microwave."

"No, I want to get you out of your room, not give you the gear to stay in there forever."

Nicholas came out with their entrée before Maxim could respond.

She set down her soup spoon. "You're not the only one to ever feel like an outcast."

"And you have?"

She nodded. "As you know, my mother is dead. I was six when she died."

"I'm so sorry. What happened?"

"She disappeared. She was supposed to pick me up from school but never made it. Her car was found abandoned by the park. It was in the news, police searched for her for months before they found her body in the river."

"My Belle. That's horrible. What happened?"

She brushed away a tear. "They don't know if she was killed, or if she…" She couldn't say the words. Belle still couldn't imagine why her mother would kill herself.

Yet, she hated the thought that she'd been killed. "I like to think it must have been an accident of some kind."

Maxim pushed away from the table and walked over to her, kneeling beside her. She couldn't see his face under his hooded cloak. He reached for her hand, rubbing it gently with his thumb. "I didn't know. I'm so sorry. My cosmetic concerns must seem so shallow to you."

She shook her head. "No, they don't. I just want you to know that I understand what it's like to feel like an outsider. People stared and whispered about me at school for a few weeks. I was the girl whose mother had been found dead in the river. I'd never felt so alone."

He squeezed her hand.

"But it didn't last forever. People forgot, or just accepted it. I could have withdrawn, knowing I was different from everyone else. But I didn't."

"They never determined what happened?"

Belle shook her head. "But I had a choice to make; live my life or be dead, like my mother. Maxim, in your own way, you are dead."

He slowly pulled his hand away from hers. "It's true. In a way, I am dead. The Prince Maxim the world knew is gone."

"It's time for the new Prince Maxim to start living. The one who understands people's pain. The one who is caring and kind. Those qualities are just as attractive as a handsome face." She squeezed his hand. "Can I see your face, Maxim?"

He was still as he sat beside her. "It seems so foolish now, after listening to your story. You were a brave young girl, and here I am, a grown man and a coward." He sighed, and slipped the hood off his head. Slowly, he raised his face to hers without looking at her.

Her throat tightened when she first saw his scars. It hurt her to see the damage that had been done to him. While his head was raised to her, his eyes were cast downward. "Max, I can't see you. Look at me."

Slowly, his lids raised.

She smiled at him. "Your eyes are beautiful." She reached her hand to touch his cheek, running her thumb across the edge of his scar. "Does it hurt?"

"No. Not anymore. But it's horrible, isn't it?"

"No, it's not. It certainly looks like something happened, but it's not shocking. It's nothing that should keep you locked in your room for eternity." She nudged him with her elbow. "Hey, some chicks dig scars."

That got a smile out of him. "But you're kind. I'm sure strangers on the street would react like I'm a monster."

She shrugged. "You might get a look or two. But so what?"

He closed his eyes and shook his head. "Coming downstairs to meet you was a big enough step for now. I don't know if I can do more than that."

"I hope you can someday. I like being here with you. But I'm not willing to be locked away. Not even with prince charming." She winked at him.

But clearly he wasn't feeling playful, because his hand slipped off her arm. "Then I'll always remember this time with you. Because my bravery, if I ever had any, has disappeared, along with my looks. You don't know what it feels like to be me." He stood up and stepped back from her.

She looked up at him. "But I do know what it feels like to be different from everyone."

He reached his hand out to her. "Come with me. There's something we need to do."

She cocked her head; surely he wasn't suggesting *that*. Although, it probably had been a while for him.

He seemed to know what she was thinking. "It's positively innocent, although Reginald probably won't approve."

"Well, if Reginald won't approve, I'm in." Standing up, she followed him, intrigued. He led her down the hall and up the stairs. "I thought you said this was innocent?" She arched an eyebrow.

"It is." He patted the banister. "I had Nicholas try it out earlier. If it can support him, it can support you."

She stared at him.

"You did say you'd slide down the banister if this was your place, didn't you?"

She laughed. "I did. I used to slide down the banister at my grandmother's house when I was little." She hesitated, eyeing it up.

"I imagine it's like riding a bike—you never forget how. Give it a go."

Taking a deep breath, she hiked up her dress, grasped the railing, and threw her leg over it. She loosened her grip and slid down the smooth, curving wood. She shrieked as she headed for the bottom.

The prince raced down the stairs and caught her at the bottom, his fingers wrapping round her waist as he lowered her to the ground. Turning her around, he brought her closer, and quickly swiped his lips across hers. He pulled back, as if waiting for her reaction. Smiling, she leaned in and met his mouth with hers.

His trembling hands cupped her face and he kissed her passionately. She gripped his shoulders, never wanting the moment to end.

A sigh slipped from her lips when he broke their kiss. "Was it everything you hoped for?" he whispered.

She nodded. "The ride down the banister was nice, too." She rested her head on his shoulder, then looked up at him. "While we're on the topic of granting my wishes, it'd be great to take a walk in the park."

She was still in his arms, but he let go and stepped back.

"Goodnight, Belle. I'm grateful you don't see the beast that peers back at me from my mirror. But I fear you're the only one able to see past it."

***

The next morning as she returned to her work, she peered into the hall, straining to hear any sound that the prince was coming to her. Perhaps she had been too forward with him, too careless with her words. She'd pushed too hard and too fast.

She heard someone coming and whirled around to face the door. Her shoulders slumped when she saw it was Nicholas. Then her heart kicked up a notch when she saw he was frowning.

"What is it?"

"Belle, the hospital's been calling you. Your father … he's taken a turn for the worse. Come. I'll drive you to the hospital."

***

She ran down the hall to his room. *This can't be happening.* She turned into his room and started shaking. Somehow, her father seemed smaller and weaker since she'd seen him two days ago. Her hand flew to her mouth. "Daddy, no!"

She knelt next to his bed, reached for his hand and started to pray.

When the doctor finally came in, he told her his vital signs were weak but stable. "The next twenty-four hours should tell us more. He's either going to pull through this, or decline. It wouldn't be long after that."

She fought back a sob and nodded as the doctor left the room. Working for the prince had been for nothing. She should have been here with her father instead of worrying about saving his job. She'd been so certain he'd pull through. Why had it never occurred to her he wouldn't? Had she let herself become so enamored with Maxim, she'd forgotten the real reason she was there in the first place?

She rested her arms on the cold metal rail of her father's bed and let the tears out.

***

Maxim paced his room. Nicholas had called him with the news and it wasn't good. Belle's father was in a

precarious condition. With no mother, she couldn't lose
her father, too. He couldn't imagine how she was feeling.
Did she even have anyone to turn to? He knew there was
no boyfriend in her life. Her friends were back upstate.
His heart pounded just thinking of it. Could he go to
her?

He closed his eyes. He couldn't. But how could
he not?

He dialed Nicholas on his cell. "Take me to the
hospital."

"To the hospital? Are you sure?"

"I have to be there for her if something happens."

"I'll be right there."

Maxim looked around the room where he'd spent
most of his last six years. "I'll be waiting in the lobby."

"Of the building?"

"Yes."

"I'll be there in ten minutes."

Maxim put on his cloak and dashed down the
stairs. Mrs. Downing froze as she watched him coming
downstairs. A huge smile split her face. "Your
highness!" Her hand fluttered over her throat.
"You're downstairs! Let me get you some milk. Some
pie? Courtney could make a pie. You always loved pie.
Tea?"

"Belle's at the hospital with her father. She needs
me."

Mrs. Downing's eyes were wide as she nodded
and watched him hurry out the door without even closing
it behind him.

He was fortunate to get the elevator to himself.
He paced impatiently as he rode slowly down to the
lobby. He'd forgotten the slow, lurching ride that left his
stomach queasy. Or maybe it was fear for Belle that had
left him feeling that way.

People passed him the lobby, but he wasn't aware
of their reactions. His cloak obscured his face, but seeing
a man in a dark, hooded cape must be disconcerting, as

well. It was of no concern to him. Nothing could keep him from her. *Please let her father pull through.*

***

Nicholas chased after him as Maxim raced down the hall. He found her father's room and paused outside of it. It hadn't occurred to him she might not want him here. It was too late. He *was* here, and he wanted her to know he cared; that he cared more about her than his own feeble insecurities. He knocked softly on the door. "Belle?"

She jumped and turned to him. Her eyes widened. "Maxim? What are you doing here?"

He walked toward her and held his arms open. "I couldn't let you be alone at a time like this. I kept thinking of you as a little girl ... and your mother." He swallowed the lump in this throat.

She folded herself into his arms. He held her tight and tried to fight back his tears. It was the closest he'd been to anyone in years and it felt like magic and dreams holding her. Maybe he hadn't come here for Belle, after all.

Maybe he needed her more than she needed him.

Belle gave him the rundown of her father's prognosis. "It's just a waiting game, now."

"Then I'll wait with you."

***

They spent the night sleeping in uncomfortable hospital chairs, waking as nurses came in to check on her father.

Nicholas returned in the morning with coffee and breakfast for them both. Maxim offered her the orange from his meal. He felt at such a loss that he couldn't do anything to help.

"I don't think I can eat. But thank you." Her face was pale and he reached for her hand.

They both turned at the sound of footsteps. Nicholas was leading a doctor into the room. "Prince

117

Maxim? This is the chief plastic surgeon on staff. He'd like to have a word with you."

The prince looked at Belle. She smiled. "Go. See what he has to say. You owe me a walk in the park." She squeezed his hand.

His heart was in his throat and his voice came out in a whisper. "I will. For you." He kissed her forehead and let go of her hand.

But Belle was shaking her head. "Don't do it for me. Do it for you."

He took a deep breath, nodded, and followed Nicholas and the doctor into the hall.

***

Belle's head was spinning with hope and fear. She was thrilled for Maxim. Her father couldn't leave her now. She grabbed his hand. "Daddy, can you hear me? I need you. There's so much ahead of us."

She wasn't sure, but she thought her father squeezed her hand. "Do that again," she whispered. And he did.

She pushed the call button for the nurse.

***

Two weeks later, her father watched her work on the last of the bookcases. "You do better work than me … my daughter." Her father was slowing regaining his speech. The prince had insisted on him recovering at Maxim's apartment. Mrs. Downing was in her glory waiting on him.

Belle looked up from the trim she was cutting. "Only on the finish work, Dad. I could never frame up a job like you do."

The prince stuck his head in the room. "Why do you insist on working? The bookshelves can wait."

She grinned at him. "I've got quite the to-do list. I've got a ballroom to remodel when I'm done here."

He frowned. "Right. I promised you a ball, didn't I?"

"So I could be—"

"The belle of the ball," he finished. He paused for a moment and ran his fingers along the bookshelves. "You've already made over this whole place, Belle, just by being here."

She blushed and looked down.

He held out his hand. "How about a walk?"

"Outside? Now?"

He nodded.

"You haven't had your first surgery yet." Doctors had planned three surgeries over the next year, but told him they'd never be able to fully correct the damage.

He smiled. "Yes. I've spent too many beautiful days inside alone."

***

He wore a hat, which shaded his face. A few people glanced his way as they walked by, but he was too busy looking at her to notice. "Where shall we go?" he asked, his three dogs pulling on the leashes he held in one hand.

She looped her arm around his and leaned into him. "The river."

He stopped walking. "Are you sure?"

She took a deep breath of the fresh air. "I am. You see, I met a brave prince who convinced me to face my own demons."

He laughed it was such a lovely sound. "Ah, so you owe me one."

"I guess I do." She pulled him along the sidewalk and started walking again, the river just around the corner. "So, how am I going to repay you?"

Taking her hands in his, he pulled her close. "Come with me when I return to my country."

She felt her eyes widen. "Move with you there?"

He laughed. "No. This is my home now. But I need to show my people I'm still alive and well. Very well. Thanks to you."

They crossed the street and she looked out over the river. She didn't know exactly where they were headed together, but she knew it would have a happy ending.

Somewhere, she'd hoped her mother was smiling. "A trip to your country? It's a date."

"Good. After that, it's back home for the ball, my Belle." And then he did something amazing, simply by taking off his hat and smiling up at the sky.

"Snow"
by Lisa Scott

Shawna White nudged past the couple kissing on the sidewalk tethered to three enormous dogs. She'd never been crazy enough about someone to stop and kiss them on the street. How sad was that? Back in high school, she and her friend, Goldie, had decided they'd know they were in love when they madly kissed someone in public. Hadn't happened so far. She wondered if it had for Goldie. Shawna liked to tell herself she was too focused on her career to care about romance, but that was just an easy excuse to soothe a lonely heart.

She kicked a stone along the sidewalk until it skittered into the street. Maybe if she landed the audition to be the voice for the new kids' juice beverage, she could stop worrying about finding work and focus on the more important things in life. However, the producers that morning hadn't given her any indication they'd been impressed with her impression of a singing bean stalk stretching to the sky, unlocking a treasure trove of fruits and veggies. Really, how does a girl channel a legume? Truth was nothing had gone right since her father died a year ago.

Taking the elevator to the modest apartment she shared with her stepmother, she crossed her fingers that something good would come her way soon. *Life shouldn't be this stagnant at age twenty-three,* she thought to herself.

She bumped the front door open with her hip, and Veronica, her stepmother, looked up from her magazine, smiling like a hawk. Nothing good ever followed *that* look. "I've got wonderful news," she said. "I've found you a job. Now you can start contributing to the rent. It may be a cheap hovel thanks to your father's business dealings, but still, there are bills to be paid."

Shaw groaned. She stopped taking her stepmother's bait soon after her father died. Veronica missed the money; Shaw missed her father. End of story. "Veronica, I just got back from an audition, and I have another one lined up tomorrow. I'll find something."

Veronica rolled her eyes. "When are you going to give up on that silly idea?"

"I'm not giving up."

"Well, this will tide you over until you get that big call. And it's urgent. The man I'm seeing needs a nanny. I can't stand one more minute watching those kids. One of the little ones has a cough." She wrinkled her nose. "I could get sick."

Shaw flopped onto the couch and stared at the ceiling. Dealing with her stepmother was more like wrangling a ridiculous older sister. She was a child pageant queen all grown up; she lived by different rules. "You do realize if you marry him, he'll expect you to help with the kids."

"No, he won't. Jeremy has agreed to take on a nanny for the children, and I recommended you."

Shaw laughed. "I have no experience as a nanny. I've never even held a baby."

"They're not babies. They can walk. And poop on their own, I think." Veronica pressed her hand against her chest. "Plus, you don't need experience when you have my recommendation. Be there tomorrow at one."

She couldn't turn down a job handed to her on a platter. She'd lost her waitress position because she'd skipped out for one too many auditions, she'd been too mortified to continue with the singing telegram gig, and she didn't have any jewelry left to pawn. It couldn't be that hard to watch a few children. Once you've worked as a singing "love bug" delivering flowers, anything would seem easy, right?

***

Shaw walked twenty blocks to Grimm Towers to save on cab fare. Jeremy James lived on the twenty-fifth floor in one of the swankiest buildings in the city; no wonder Veronica was chasing him. Once upon a time, Shaw's father had been just as wealthy. But then he lost his money in a Ponzi scheme. Not too long after that, he died. That was over a year ago. Veronica had been scrambling for a new husband ever since. Not so easy to do once you hit thirty, Veronica was learning.

Standing in the lobby, Shaw sucked in a breath, certain she wouldn't be applying for a job she didn't want if her parents were alive. Her mother died when she was a child. If she'd grown up without knowing the real love of a mother, did she have any hope of properly caring for little kids?

She jabbed the elevator button again, like she could leave her sad memories in the lobby if only she could get on the elevator. She tapped her foot and crossed her arms.

A nanny. Could I be a nanny? Shaw was an only child, so it's not like she had experience with siblings. Or cousins. Or kids in general, for that matter. But she did need a job. And with her voice training had come a bit of acting. She could pull this off. She had to convince Jeremy she was up to the task of watching his children. It couldn't be that hard. Millions of people did it every day. Then, once she landed an audition, she could move on.

When she found his apartment, she rang the bell and

just about dropped her purse when the door opened. A tall, handsome man with auburn hair, flecked with gray, smiled at her. Shaw hadn't been expecting this. Veronica wasn't fussy about looks, so long as the man had money. A handsome face was just a bonus. Veronica must have been thinking 'jackpot' with this one. And he was younger than she'd expected. He appeared to be in his thirties. Her father had been fifty when he'd married Veronica.

Shaw called her up best professional-laced-with-a-splash-of-sex-voice. It worked in most situations. "Mr. James? I'm Shawna White."

He held out his hand. "Nice to meet you. I'm so glad you're interested in the job. It's not easy to find someone willing to work with seven children." The corners of his eyes crinkled as he grinned.

Shaw stepped back and willed her smile to stay in place. "I'm sorry, you said seven children?"

He rubbed his chin. "Ah. Veronica didn't tell you. No wonder you showed up."

Veronica came up behind him and set her hand on his arm. "I'm sure I mentioned that, Shawna. How he has this wonderful little…." She circled a hand in the air searching for the right word. "Little mob of kids. A pack of them. They're a tiny gang." She shrugged and giggled.

Shaw clapped her hands together in mock enthusiasm. "Guess I didn't hear you, Veronica. That's fine, the more the merrier. Let's meet them."

He led her inside and cupped his hands around his mouth. "Kids? Come out to the living room and meet my new friend."

A sound like a stampede of miniature horses filled

the room. She gulped. Three tiny blond boys rushed for their daddy's knees, nearly knocking him over. They were followed by two curly-haired girls, half a foot taller, holding hands and skipping behind them.

An older boy and girl rounded out the group; the boy with his nose in a book, the girl rolling her eyes. They were the same height, with straight, reddish-brown hair like their father. "Is that everyone?" Shaw asked, fearful there could be more.

His mouth opened, but before he could answer, three cats, two birds, a ferret and a little dog tumbled into the room. Shaw gasped.

"And we've got a few pets, too," Jeremy said, rubbing the back of his head.

Shaw rocked back on her heels. "That's no problem." Right? Animals were easy. Although, she'd never had a pet of her own. Well, a goldfish when she was twelve that lasted three days before she fed it to death. *Mental note: must not give the children too much food.*

"So, let's start with the triplets." Jeremy pulled the three identical platinum-haired boys in front of him and tousled their heads. "This is Jordan, John, and Jake. Just turned three years old a few weeks ago."

She flapped her hand at them. "Hi, guys. You look just like Daddy."

They beamed up at her, while two cats wound themselves between their legs. "We're this many." Jake held up four fingers.

"Close, honey." She folded down one of his fingers. "You're this many." Clearly, they'd need some help with their math.

Jeremy smiled at them, his adoration for the little guys evident in his grin. "Go sit on the couch, boys."

The curly-haired girls took their place, like they'd

been through this drill before. "Meet the twins, Maddie and Jenny," he said, putting an arm around each girl.

"Don't worry. We're much more mature than them." One of the girls looked over at the triplets wrestling on the couch.

Her twin nodded in agreement. "We're six, and we're also very intelligent. I'm Jenny."

"And I'm Maddie. How do you know Daddy?"

"She's Veronica step-daughter," he said.

Jenny nodded and looked at Veronica. "So, that means you're her mommy now?"

Veronica laughed. "Oh, no, no, no. Nooo. I'm too young to be someone's mother. Look at me. Do I look like a mother?"

Maddie smiled up at her. "You're the prettiest lady I know."

Veronica didn't even bat an eye. "Thank you sweetie. I just hit my thirties."

Shaw planted her hand on her hip. "Really? Because I was sixteen when you married my father and I remember thinking, eww, she's only eleven years older than me. So that would make you thirty-four now."

Veronica didn't look quite as pretty when her face was red. But she quickly recovered, and forced a big smile. "Well, it *feels* like I just hit the thirties. Sometimes I forget. Time goes by so quickly, doesn't it, Jeremy?" Flipping her hair over her shoulder, she beamed at him.

"It does. I can't believe I'm thirty-five already. With seven kids," he said, incredulously.

Veronica's eyes widened and she blinked at him. This must have been news to her. For once, she was chasing a man her age.

One of his older kids cleared their throat. "Dad,

are you forgetting us? You know, your first born?"

"Ah, yes. My first set of twins, Lizzy and Tyler. Lizzy can keep them all in line when needed, but we've been struggling to find the perfect nanny. We've gone through sitters galore. Some kind stranger in the building kept sending us food from a catering company and sitters from an agency, but they all quit. If Veronica thinks you might be the right one, I'm listening."

He explained how they mostly needed help in the morning when the kids get ready for school, and again after school, and then at bedtime. "The triplets are in day care, so once we've got them out the door, you've got some time to yourself."

She let out the breath she'd been holding. "Good, because I go on auditions from time to time."

That caught Lizzy's attention. "Auditions? For what?"

"For singing and dancing." Shaw did a quick shuffle step.

The triplets applauded. "Again! Again!"

Ah, so she had an in. "Maybe later. And if you're really good, I'll teach you how to whistle *The Star Spangled Banner* while standing on your head." That particular talent had landed her a spot in a commercial, and it had the rapt attention right now of seven little kids. "Oh, and the bunny hop. Do you guys know how to do the bunny hop?"

Seven wide-eyed children stared at her, shaking their heads.

Jeremy folded his arms. "What happens if you land an audition? Would you have to leave us?"

Veronica laughed, wrinkling her nose. "I don't think we need to worry about that. Dreams very rarely come true."

Shaw bit her tongue. "It is very competitive out there. But it depends. Sometimes, I'm auditioning for a one shot deal, like a commercial, so that would just mean a day or two off. I'd love to land a spot in a musical, or a touring production, but hundreds of the most talented dancers in the city show up for those." She shrugged. "Like Veronica said, it's a long shot."

"I guess we can cross that bridge when we come to it." Jeremy smiled at her. "Oh, and of course, free room and board is included."

Veronica's eyes widened and her voice raised an octave in pitch. "She'll be living here with you? You didn't mention that."

Jeremy shrugged. "Of course. It'd be too much of a hassle for her, otherwise."

Veronica set her hand on Shaw's shoulder. "Maybe you should take some time to think about this, Shawna."

Only Veronica insisted on calling her by her full name. She must have a list of things she could do to annoy Shaw hidden somewhere. But annoying Veronica by taking the job would be a wonderful payback for years of insults and snide remarks. Shaw fluttered her fingers, thinking it over.

Jeremy turned to the kids. "What do you say, should we try her out?"

"Yeah!" they shouted.

At that, panic swelled in her chest. "What about references? I have to be honest. I haven't worked as a nanny before."

He waved away her concern. "We're a little desperate. And Veronica is a good friend. I trust her judgment."

Veronica looked just as surprised as Shaw was to hear that declaration. Friend? Surely Veronica had thought it was something more. Oh, what was the word to describe what Shaw was feeling? Schadenfreude? Glee? Because Veronica did not deserve a man like Jeremy.

"Alright. Let's take her on a test run." He turned to Shaw. "What do you say we go to the zoo and we'll see how things go?"

"I guess I could manage in these sandals," Veronica said, inspecting her shoes. "But they are very expensive Jiminies."

"You don't have to come, Veronica. I know how you feel about places like the zoo. Let me spend some time with the kids and Shaw and see how we do together."

Shaw recognized the pinched, painful look on Veronica's face. "Of course, Jeremy. I'll see you tomorrow?"

"That's okay. I know you're busy, and now that Shaw's here, I won't need your help as much. You've been such a great friend the last year. I'm so lucky you got in touch after Dina died. I didn't realize you two had been such good friends in college."

"Yes, I miss her terribly. I'm sure she'd be pleased I was here with you now."

Shaw tried to not to roll her eyes. Veronica had taken one class with Jeremy's wife and had spotted her name in the obituary column. But clearly, Veronica wouldn't be deterred by his declaration of their friendship. "I'll give Shaw time to get settled in and then I'll give you a call. It's time we got to know each other better."

Jeremy didn't answer. While he dashed off to search for sweaters and shoes, Veronica gathered her things and gripped Shaw's arm. "Ruin this for me, and I'll kill you."

Shaw blinked at her. "I'm just here for the kids." Then she yanked her arm away. "And you were the one who insisted I take this job. But now that I'm going to be living here, I guess I don't need to pitch in with the rent."

You couldn't actually see steam blowing out of a person's ears, could you?

Jeremy approached them. "Ready, Shaw?"

Veronica's fake sun-shiney smile was back and she leaned into him, so that he could plant a kiss on her lips if he wanted. But he patted her on the back, instead. "Thanks, again, Veronica."

***

"Okay, kids. Let's leave the polar bears alone. There are other things to see," Jeremy said.

"No! I want to see them belly flop. I saw them do that once and I'm waiting till they do it again," six-year-old Maddie said, her hands on her hips and bottom lip protruding.

"We've been watching them for half an hour," Lizzie complained.

Jeremy looked up at the sky. "It's times like this I especially miss their mother."

They had to get this question out of the way; she might as well do it now. "What happened?" Veronica had told her his wife had died and that she had hideous hair in college, but didn't bother with the specifics. Of the death, not the hair. Veronica had gone into great detail about the bad hair.

He sighed, and gripped the railing in front of them. "She was in a car accident. She'd just dropped the triplets off at day care and was on her way to work. We think she fell asleep at the wheel. We weren't getting much sleep back then."

She touched his arm. "I'm so sorry. For all of you."

He nodded. "I try my best for them, but I just can't do it myself."

"I'll do whatever I can to help." She didn't even have to fake sounding sincere; she meant it. Although, when she turned to round up the kids, nerves bubbled through her. There were so many of them. And they didn't stand still. And they were never quiet. *Desperate times.* She stuck two fingers in her mouth and whistled.

The giggling and wriggling stopped.

"Whoa," John said. "You're just like Thomas the Tank Engine."

"You're right. I am. So get behind me and let's move this James family train to the giraffe exhibit." She marched in place and bent her arms, rotating them like the axles on a train.

The kids laughed and hurried to line up behind her.

Jeremy nodded in approval. "Line up like a train. Why didn't I think of that?"

"You probably didn't star in your third grade production of *The Little Engine That Could*, did you?"

"Nope. You got me there. See, you're more qualified than you thought."

With hands on the hips of the person in front of them, the conga line of kids shuffled their way to the giraffes.

Of course, then they wanted to travel like that the rest of their trip. So they waddled like penguins. They strutted like ducks, and marched like soldiers.

When they got back to Jeremy's apartment, they didn't want her to leave. "You've got the job if you want it, Shaw."

And surprisingly, she wanted it. She really did. "Great."

"I'll send the movers to pick up your things tomorrow."

***

Veronica ground her teeth the entire cab ride home. It would probably be the subway from here on out, now that she couldn't count on any rent help from Shawna. Ugh. How had this blown up in her face? She dug her nails into her Prada bag, the last real one she owned. The rest were fakes. Shawna working as a nanny was supposed to mean more time for Jeremy to get to know Veronica. Not loads of time for him to spend with Shawna.

Veronica tucked her long, blond hair behind her ears. Those highlights cost her two hundred fifty dollars a month. Plus tip. Botox was another three hundred. Eyelash extensions were two hundred a month. It wasn't easy or cheap being beautiful. But it was important. Shawna did very little with herself. The girl didn't even wax her eyebrows. Veronica curled her upper lip in disgust—her recently bleached upper lip.

True, Shawna was younger than Veronica, but Jeremy certainly couldn't find her attractive, could he? Her skin was almost as white as milk. With the contrast of her dark black hair, she practically looked like a ghost. Or a corpse. It had never crossed Veronica's mind to worry about Shawna as a competitor before.

But she hadn't realized Shawna would be invited to

live there. Or that Jeremy would go to the zoo with
them. Why couldn't Shawna have taken the kids by
herself so Veronica could get to spend time with Jeremy?
That was the whole point of this venture. To move
things along and become Mrs. Jeremy James. True, he
would be her third husband, but one didn't need to
count. Then she'd be living in the same apartment
building as her mother, and she'd be welcomed back with
open arms once she landed her man.

Her mother's words tickled the edges of her
memory. "Don't worry about your school work,
Veronica. The best thing you can do is find yourself a
rich husband."

And despite all her protests, all her work in college to
be something more than a scheming harpy like her
mother, here she was on the very same path. What do
they say about the apple and the tree?

The cab stopped in front of her apartment building.
"Twenty-one fifty-six," said the cabbie.

Veronica panicked, and looked in her wallet. She
had a twenty-dollar bill and two quarters. Taking a deep
breath, she lifted one shoulder and curled her mouth into
a smile. "Silly, silly me. I'm short about a dollar. Can
you help a girl out? You seem like the sort who knows
how to take care of a woman."

And as he accepted her reduced payment with a
smile, she stepped out into the cold, gray day realizing her
mother had been right all along. Finding a rich man was
Veronica's best bet.

And her whiny little stepdaughter better not get in
her way of this one.

***

Three weeks later, Shawna was in love with her job.

Gah, and her boss, too. Jeremy was so funny and thoughtful and fun, she forgot how handsome he was. The James family train method of maintaining order was holding strong, and she'd even tricked the kids into helping her clean up by making it a race. "Who can pick up and put away ten toys the fastest?" she'd challenge them. "I bet Jenny can!" And oh, the race that ensued left the place spotless.

She even liked the darn animals. The parrot enjoyed perching on her shoulder and twining its beak in her hair, while the cats followed her around the apartment and curled up at her feet whenever she paused to sit down. Which wasn't often.

She was so busy and so happy working for Jeremy and his kids, she'd skipped a few auditions. In fact, she hadn't been on one since the day she first met the James family. And she wasn't even upset that she didn't get the part of the dancing clock in the sleep medication commercial she'd auditioned for a few weeks back. But she did find herself singing all the time; and she only sang when she was happy.

As she sat coloring with the kids, she realized the only thing keeping this job from being perfect was Veronica. She wasn't giving up on Jeremy, so she was around a lot. Questioning Shaw's decision to give the kids string cheese for a snack. "What about a nice brie?" she'd suggested. And now, criticizing her crayon drawings as rather juvenile for a twenty-three year old. Shaw pressed so hard on the crayon it broke.

Veronica snickered. "You must have skipped pastels in performing arts school."

Shaw finished the purple and pink drawing of a unicorn Jenny had requested, and signed her name at the bottom. "No. I was so talented in crayons, they exempted me from the course."

Maddie grabbed the picture from her and squinted at it. "Snow?"

Shaw rolled her eyes. "It says 'Shaw.' S-H-A-W."

Jenny stood next to her sister shaking her head. "It looks like S-N-O-W. The bar on your H is too short. And the A is missing its tail."

"You guys are tough," Shaw said.

"Guess you didn't take handwriting, either," Veronica said.

"Snow!" Jake said. "Your name is Snow."

"Your skin is as white as snow," Veronica offered. "Haven't you ever heard of spray tanning?"

"Don't you have somewhere else to be? Jeremy's busy working and we've got things under control here." The way Shaw saw it, Jeremy didn't seem to be encouraging her. But he wasn't discouraging her, either. He went to a lot of charity events, and Veronica was the perfect go-to date. And that was enough to keep her in the game.

"Don't wait up for us!" she'd told Shaw last Friday when they went to some charity auction. But they were home by ten.

And since Jeremy worked from home, Veronica stopped by a lot. Shaw was seeing more of her now than when they lived in the same apartment.

As subtle as the scent of her heavily applied, insanely expensive perfume, Veronica picked up her bridal magazine and was leafing through it, when Jeremy came out of his office. "I've got to go to an event for the zoo this Saturday night. Are you busy?" he asked Veronica.

"Let me check my schedule." She pulled out her

phone, tapped the screen and shrugged. "Looks like I'm open."

"Great. Can you watch the kids? I thought I'd take Shawna since you don't really like animals. The event is being held among the zoo displays. I know you probably wouldn't want to get your Jiminies dirty."

Veronica's jaw hung open. Then she snapped it shut and laughed in a high-pitched giggle. "Of course! You think I can't handle the kids?"

He turned to Shaw. "Is that okay with you, Shaw? Would you like to come?"

"Of course. I love animals. And I'd hate for Veronica to suffer through it." She looked at her. "Guess you owe me one."

Veronica said nothing, but Shaw could see her hands gripping the edge of the couch, her knuckles white.

"Actually, could you keep an eye on them right now? I want Shaw's opinion on the logo I just created for a new client."

"Daddy, her name is Snow. Look at how she signed her drawing," Jenny said, with her hand on her hip.

Jeremy looked at the picture and chuckled. "Kinda like Madonna, huh? A one-name wonder. Alright, Snow, let me show you what I've worked up."

Shaw thought about ducking so the daggers from Veronica's eyes had no chance of hitting her. Veronica hadn't been given a nickname.

Leading her to his office, Jeremy sat down in front of his computer, and brought up the image. "It's for the Naughty and Nice bakery."

Identical twin cupcake girls, one dressed as a vixen, the other as a demure maiden smiled at her. She laughed, sitting next to him. "I like it."

"Good. Ideas have been coming to me so much quicker now that you're here."

She raised an eyebrow. "Seriously?"

He stretched back in his chair, lacing his hands behind his head. "For the first time in a long time, I can relax and focus. I know you've got things under control. I can trust you. We're lucky to have you here, Shaw."

"I'm really happy to be here."

"You know, you don't have to do all the cooking. I've been meaning to hire a chef. We've been living on takeout since ... since Dina died. She was a great cook." He sat forward and looked over at her. "But you are too."

She smoothed her hands down her thighs. "I didn't even know I enjoyed cooking. I don't mind. Really. Maddie and Jenny like helping me."

They were shoulder to shoulder and her belly flipped hearing this praise from him. Oh, she was so cliché, feeling lust like this for her boss. Bad made-for-TV movies used this device as a plot starter. What would he do if he knew how she felt? Would he fire her? She'd grown to love the kids. She wouldn't be chasing their daddy and mess things up.

Get over it, sister. She stood up. "Did you want to go grab lunch with Veronica?" Boy, did it suck saying that. But if he were taken, she wouldn't be dreaming about him, right?

"No, I'm not hungry."

"I think she is." She hoped the double entrendre was noticeable in her delivery.

He cocked his head. "What are you saying?"

She turned her hands up and shrugged. "She's here a lot."

"She was Dina's friend. She's here for her."

- Shaw raised an eyebrow. "It's not exactly like you need her help now. But she keeps coming."

"Hmm." He rubbed his chin. "Maybe she feels put out."

The man was clueless. But dating was probably the last thing on his mind. Maybe a night babysitting the kids would send Veronica packing. "What should I wear Saturday?"

"It's formal. I'll pay for a gown. My wife had an account at the shop down the street. Pick out something and have them bill me." He turned back to his computer, then looked at her. "Oh, and Dina used to stop at the Diva salon beforehand. Feel free if you'd like. It's on me. I really appreciate this."

"No problem." *I'll just be worrying about it all week.*

***

Veronica was not going to pout about this anymore. If Jeremy liked his new help, it was time to get rid of her. She knew plenty of people who could get Shawna out of the picture. Pacing the apartment, she pulled out a cigarette and inhaled slowly, waiting for the nicotine to calm her. Rarely did she allow herself the indulgence. She could handle this, but who was the right person to call?

With a snap of her fingers, Veronica popped open her laptop. Mark Hunt had the right background, and hopefully he remembered that embarrassing photo she still had of him from their days in college. Trying on her lingerie probably seemed like a lark at the time, but now, it was her golden ticket. Stubbing the cigarette out, she felt much better.

After a quick Internet search, she found him, pleased he was still working in video production. She dialed his number and got him on the first ring. "Mark? It's Veronica Midas. How are you darling? I was hoping we could meet up this Friday. I have a teensy little favor to ask of you. And old photos to share, of course."

***

Shawna's fingers trembled during the cab ride to the lunch meeting that would change her life. She just couldn't believe her luck. Or maybe she should call it her bad luck; she'd have to leave the James family. But the opportunity of a lifetime had just landed in her lap. She'd dropped the triplets off at day care, before dashing off this interview. She hadn't mentioned it to Jeremy.

The owner of a video production company was looking to cast someone as the host of a ten-week reality dating show touring the country called, "In Search Of Prince Charming." Mark Hunt had gotten a copy of her audition tape from a friend in the business, and thought she was perfect. He apologized for the hasty interview, but apparently, the woman they'd hired was a diva who just wasn't working out. Once the paperwork was signed, she'd have to leave for the tour in two days. The crew was already in Boston, filming, and she'd join them there. This meeting was just to formalize the details.

If she decided to take the job.

She paid the driver, took a deep breath, and tried to erase the image of seven beautiful children from her mind. This was her dream, and she'd finally made it. She walked into the restaurant and told the hostess she was meeting Mark Hunt.

"Right this way," she said, leading her to a table.

This is really happening! She smoothed her hands down her skirt.

Mark stood up and introduced himself, and Shawna

liked him immediately. He was in his thirties, and dressed in an expensive suit. She'd googled his company and read incredible things about Golden Egg productions.

She shook his hand, "It's so mice to neet you," she said, then plopped in her seat, mortified. "I mean, it's so *nice* to *meet* you. I have to admit, I'm really nervous. This is such an incredible opportunity. I can't believe how lucky I am." She grinned at him, hoping she seemed more enthusiastic than desperate and pathetic.

He frowned for a moment, then forced a smile, and she wondered if she'd blown it. "I'm just glad you're going to be able to fill in on such short notice," he said. They ordered drinks, and he got right down to the details of the job—and the incredible salary—and the opportunities this would no doubt bring her.

"So what do you think?" he asked.

She twisted her napkin in her lap. "I'd have to leave a fantastic job I have right now. I'm a nanny to seven wonderful kids. I'd hate to leave them. They lost their mother last year, but how could I pass this up? I've been dreaming of this kind of opportunity since I was little." She sat on her hands to keep them still. "One of my few memories of my mother is dancing with her. She was a ballerina, but then she developed cancer. She wrote me a letter before she died, telling told me I'd grow up to do great things."

Mark looked down.

Maybe she was revealing too much, but she couldn't stop now. Shaw pressed her eyes shut, hoping to keep back the tears. "She'd be so proud to see me on TV." She blew out a breath and looked at him. Why was she hesitating? She had to take this job; but something was holding her back. "I just wish my father were still alive to talk this over with." She stared out the window, wishing her heart would give her the right answer. Would she regret it forever if she passed this up?

Mark sighed and set down his drink. "Hell, I didn't look horrible in that bustier," he mumbled.

"Excuse me?"

He shook his head. "Nothing. The offer's off the table."

She sat up. "What? Why?" She shouldn't have hesitated. He was probably questioning her commitment.

"I can't do this to you, kid," he said.

"What do you mean?"

He shifted in his seat, looking around the room. "You have to promise not to say anything to Veronica. She set this up, there is no job, she just wanted to get you away from the man you're nannying for. I owed her a favor, and said I'd offer you a position that would force you to quit and leave town." He sighed. "I'm sorry. You're too nice to do this to. Don't tell her I tipped you off. Just tell her you wouldn't take it, okay? I don't know what you did to her, but watch yourself."

Her heart tumbled, but luckily the anger in her gut kept the tears from falling, too. "Thanks for being honest with me. I'll keep this between you and me." She pushed away from the table, wondering why Veronica hated her so much.

***

Veronica showed up at Jeremy's bright and early the next morning. Hopefully, Shawna had already packed up her things and left for Boston, and Veronica would be there to save the day.

But then Shaw answered the door.

Veronica felt her smile fall. "What are you doing here?"

"Nannying, like I always do. Why? Did you expect me to be somewhere else?"

"No. Not at all. Why would I think that? I was just stopping by. I thought you'd be taking the children to day care, that's all." *Good recovery*, she thought to herself.

"We don't leave for another hour." Shaw stepped aside so Veronica could come in. "Actually," Shaw said, "I was offered a fabulous job touring the country as the host of a dating show. Just out of the blue! Imagine my luck."

"What wonderful news! When do you leave?"

Shawna shook her head. "I just love my position here so much, I couldn't take it.

Veronica froze, as an icy chill shot through her. "Why not? Why ever wouldn't you take it? It's everything you've ever wanted!"

Shawna folded her arms and smiled at her. "Maybe what I've wanted has changed. And it's all thanks to you setting me up with this job. I really like the kids. And Jeremy, too. He's out, by the way."

Veronica pursed her lips, turned on her heel and marched down the hall.

She waited until she got home to scream. Then she composed herself. If she couldn't get rid of the nanny, then she'd just have to out-nanny her. "A determined Midas woman is an unbeatable foe," she said, repeating her mother's words.

***

That Saturday night, with her hair in a ponytail (that she slaved over for half an hour to get just so) Veronica put on her yoga pants and a comfortable shirt so she could dance and sing and play and do whatever else the little hellions wanted to do. Maybe she'd wear the kids out so they'd go to bed early. *No, I want Jeremy to see me interacting with them when he gets home.* Panic swelled in her chest. What if he had fun with Shawna? What if they stayed out late? Jeremy usually rushed home before eleven to be sure the kids were okay.

Veronica showed up half an hour early, hoping for a little alone time before they went out. She shouldn't be upset by this. He was being thoughtful by not inviting her to a place where she'd feel uncomfortable. She felt better as she waited to be let in.

But then Shawna opened the door in a stunning lilac gown with her hair pulled up off her slender neck. Someone who knew what they were doing had made up her face. Veronica forced a smile. "Is that what you're wearing?"

Shawna looked down and smoothed her hands over her hips. "This isn't good?"

"Oh, I'm sure you'll be fine. No one will pay you any mind." She pushed past her and walked into the apartment. "Now where are my favorite children in the whole wide world?

"I'm not sure, but Jeremy's kids are in the playroom."

Veronica narrowed her eyes at her then stalked off down the hall. "Kids? I'm here. Who's ready to have some super-duper fun? We're going to play games and make crafts and…" God. What else do people do with kids? She just hoped Jeremy was nearby to hear this interaction with the children.

"Good, you're here," he said, walking down the hall adjusting his cuff links. She sucked in a breath. The man was so handsome. That used to be her top priority in a guy—good looks. But then her job as a marketing assistant had her landlord pounding on her door every month because her rent was late. When he gave her the eviction notice she had three choices: find a cheaper apartment, which would be impossible—she was already at the bottom of the barrel; find a roommate—not gonna happen; or find a man to take care of her like her mother had advised her all along. God, she hated when her mother was right.

She'd thrown up the day she quit her job to marry her first husband. But then she'd never looked back. She'd been blessed with good looks and brains, but the brains hadn't gotten her far enough. It was time for plan B—her mother's plan.

And once she'd decided the working world wasn't for her and her best chance was to land a man, she'd convinced herself looks didn't matter. A handsome bank account was the important thing.

But Jeremy? Her mother would love Jeremy; he had both. She wondered if her mother had seen him in the building. How long was it going to take to land this man? Mother would be so proud of her once she did.

She straightened her shoulders and smiled at Jeremy. "I can't wait to spend some time with the kids."

"Good. I think they're looking forward to it, too."

She couldn't help notice the way he escorted Shaw out the door with his hand on her lower back. He rarely did that to her. When he brushed a tendril of hair off Shaw's face, Veronica marched into the playroom to show these kids the best damn time they'd ever seen.

***

"But I don't want to color!" Jake stomped his foot, ran to his room, and locked the door.

She slumped against the wall. *Fine. One less to watch.*

"Jenny? Maddie? How about those makeovers I promised?"

They dropped the dolls they were coloring with Sharpies and followed Veronica to the dining room where she'd set a big mirror on the table, along with lipsticks and nail polish, four different kinds of hair spray and all the other ammunition she had to look as good as she did. "You girls always say how pretty I am, how would you like to look like me?"

"Yes, yes!" they cried together.

Veronica sat down in front of the mirror to reapply her lipstick. "Let me show what I use, then we'll put it on you, okay?"

"Okay," they said in singsong.

She popped open her favorite berry-colored lipstick and swiped it across her top lip. She looked at herself in the mirror and smiled. "Who's the prettiest lady in the whole wide world?" she asked. She loved hearing them say, 'You are, you are!' She went to work on her bottom lip while waiting for their answer.

Jenny looked at Maddie and shrugged. "Snow. Snow White is."

The lipstick trailed off her lip. "You mean Shawna? Shaw?"

They nodded enthusiastically. "We like to call her Snow."

She tried to force a smile, but couldn't. "You're teasing me, aren't you, you naughty girls?"

The twins shook their heads.

Veronica gulped. "You think she's prettier than me?"

"We used to think you were the prettiest, but Snow has prettier hair, and her face doesn't have those lines

145

around her eyes."

What was she getting botox for if these twerps could still see her wrinkles?

"And she sings so pretty and we just like her a lot."

Veronica slammed her makeup case shut and turned the mirror around. "I think we're all done with our makeovers for tonight."

"Aww. Please?"

"No." And with that, plans to make cookies were canceled, as was story time, and the board game. She sat the children on the couch and gave them each a book to read while she raided the kitchen for chocolate.

Snow White. Ugh. They had a nickname for her! And this was all her fault suggesting Shawna work here.

After eating half a bag of ancient chocolate chips, she slumped on the couch, flicked on a movie for the children—without any popcorn—and fell asleep.

***

Shaw was so nervous being around so many beautiful, well-dressed people, she spent the entire night at Jeremy's side. She wondered if any of them had known her father. Probably. This is the kind of event he went to from time to time. Hell, this is probably where he'd met the thief who'd convinced him to invest in the Magic Bean coffee company. He'd lost most of his money when the scam was uncovered two years later.

Jeremy looked at her and smiled. "This really isn't your kind of thing, is it?"

She wrinkled her nose. "It's not. Sorry."

"Don't be sorry. It's not my thing, either. But it's a great place to meet new clients. I think I've done enough networking tonight, though." He stood up and held out his hand. "Come on. Let's go look at the animals."

"Should I find some other people to line up and walk like a penguin?" She stuck her hands out at her side and shuffled a few steps.

He laughed. "No, just you and me this time."

That sent her heart tumbling into her stomach. "Not the reptile house. That might freak me out at night."

"Let's go see what the polar bears are up to." He set his hand on her lower back again, and that set off another round of shivers.

The moon was full and the night was chilly. Shaw tightened the shawl around her shoulders. Jeremy noticed and wrapped his arm around her. "This has been a really nice night. I love watching you with the kids, but getting to talk to you without cartoons in the background or three children hanging on my leg is nice for a change."

"You're going to have quite a few more busy years with those kiddos."

He stopped and stared at her. "I certainly hope not all by myself."

She beamed at him. "I don't plan on going anywhere anytime soon."

He ran his finger down her cheek. "I'm sure it's only a matter of time before you land one of those auditions."

She shrugged, hoping he didn't notice the shiver that had nothing to do with the cold and everything to do with his soft touch. "It would have to be something pretty special to get me to leave." She knew that now, after Veronica's little scheme. But would she say no to all offers?

"Good. We like having you around."

She felt herself frown at the word 'we.'

He noticed, tipping her chin up with one finger. "I mean, *I* like having you around. Even if I didn't have the kids, I'd like having you around." He sighed and looked up at the moon. "I'm so bad at this." He ran his hand through his hair. "Is there anyway to make this work between us? Or is it too difficult because of the kids?"

"You'd be willing to take the risk? If it didn't work out, I can't imagine I'd be able to stay on as the nanny." She looked down.

"I've thought about that. But I think finding someone to love is even harder than finding a nanny. Especially when you've got seven children to love, too."

She raised her face to his. "I'd say it's worth a chance." And as her heart thudded, he bent down and brushed his lips against hers. She kissed him back, thinking of that couple smooching in the street. She'd kiss Jeremy in the middle of rush hour traffic. Then Shaw frowned, imagining a semi running her down.

"What is it?" he asked.

"Veronica," she whispered. "She's going to be livid."

He sighed. "I was too stupid to see she was interested. I just thought she was being a good friend. I was too numb to notice anything. But she'll understand, right?"

Shaw blinked a few times. "Sure. Maybe." *Never.*

***

Jeremy kissed her one more time before they went in the apartment. "Let's not tell her tonight," Shaw said. She wanted to be sure all the knives in the house were hidden.

"Okay." He unlocked the door and led her inside. "I usually don't get home this late. It's after midnight." She followed him into the living room where Veronica was sprawled across the couch with the triplets asleep on the other end. John and Lizzie were snuggled up on a chair, and Jenny and Maddie were asleep on the floor.

"I guess they conked each other out," Shaw said.

Veronica stirred on the couch and opened her eyes. "Oh, you're home already." She sat up, smoothing her hair and tugging down her shirt. "I guess we had so much fun we just dozed off."

Jenny and Maddie woke up and rubbed their eyes. "Daddy!" They launched themselves at him and grabbed his legs.

"Did you have fun with Veronica?" he asked.

Jenny stuck out her lower lip. "No. She got mad and wouldn't give us makeovers."

He frowned. "What did you two do to her?"

"We said Snow was prettier than she is and she got really, really angry."

Veronica popped up from the couch. "What? Oh, no, no, no girls. You must have misunderstood me."

The twins glared at her with their hands on their hips. "Did not. You said—"

"Oh, who can remember what we said?" Veronica interrupted. "Now let's get you into bed."

"That's okay, Veronica. We've got it." Jeremy turned to Shaw. "I'll get the triplets, you want to handle the rest?"

"Sure."

Jeremy reached out and squeezed her hand. Veronica's eyes widened, then narrowed. "Jeremy, I promised the children I'd make them dinner tomorrow. Shall I stop by at five?"

Jeremy looked at Shaw. "Sure. We have some things to talk about."

"Good. It'll be a dinner for the ages." She scooped

up her makeup in the dining room and let herself out. "See you tomorrow." The door slammed behind her.

"We'll tell her about us tomorrow after dinner, when the kids are in bed."

"It won't be pretty."

He kissed her again and grinned. "No, not as pretty as you. I have to agree with the kids."

She bopped him with a throw pillow from the couch.

***

Veronica could very easily panic over this, but she chose not to. She was moving on to another strategy: making Shaw look bad. She'd show off her cooking skills, and maybe even set up Shaw to have a few accidents with the children. Her mind was concocting all sorts of ideas—missed appointments, lost shoes, and hell, maybe even lost kids. Veronica wasn't stupid. She'd graduated Magna Cum Laude from college. She'd told Shaw's father not to invest in that Magic Bean company. The numbers just didn't add up. But he didn't listen to her, and he'd lost them almost everything.

But she was Veronica Midas. She would land another man, and that man was going to be Jeremy James.

***

Veronica remembered making a chicken potpie with the cook one weekend when she was a child. She'd make two of them, and then a big apple pie. She made a trip to the market to buy the ingredients, and tried on five different outfits before settling on a simple, but elegant dress. Then she splurged on a cab ride to Grimm Towers where she was in the fight of her life.

Shaw was playing Twister with the kids when Jeremy let her in. "You really don't have to do this. You told me you hate cooking," he said, taking the grocery bags from her.

She pressed her hand against her chest. "Oh, no. I meant I hate cooking for just me. But cooking for all these hungry little mouths? What a dream. I hope they like chicken pot pie and apple pie?

"You're making pies for dinner?" Tyler asked. "That's odd."

"Just wait and see. Now run off and play with the nanny and let me get started on our delicious meal."

She unwrapped the frozen crusts and then stirred up the ingredients for the filling: cream of mushroom soup, peas, carrots and onions. Yuck, then she had to cut up the chicken. She plopped the meat out of its Styrofoam container onto the counter, trying her best not to gag at the site of raw meat. She pulled a big knife out of the butcher block and cut the chicken into small chunks and sautéed them.

Once she had the two potpies in the oven, she got to work on the apple pie. Luckily, Jeremy had two ovens. Was that why? One for dinner, one for dessert? Oh, it didn't matter. She wouldn't be cooking much once they were married, but it was important he knew that she could in a pinch.

She grabbed the knife again, and sliced up the apples. She didn't care so much what the apples inside the pie looked like. She cut the apples into bits and chunks and then cut a few pretty slices to garnish the top when the pie was out. She actually enjoyed the process of combining the ingredients, knowing she'd be creating something beautiful and delicious in the end. Maybe she would cook occasionally once they were married. Just for fun. She slid the pies in the oven, and soon the smells of the chicken potpie and the apples and cinnamon mingled in the apartment, which would certainly lure Jeremy into the kitchen.

"Smells good," Shawna said, walking in.

"I'm good at many things, you know. I'll call you when it's ready."

Shawna squatted down and peered in the oven. "That'll be a first. I've never had your cooking before."

She ignored Shawna. Whatever little crush Jeremy had on his nanny wouldn't last long. Veronica was setting the stage for him to tumble into her arms. A good meal would help the cause. "I'll go call the kids for dinner."

Soon, the children, Jeremy, and Shaw were seated at the table. Veronica set out the chicken potpies on the table. "We're having pie for dinner?" Maddie asked. "That can't be good for us."

Never liked that one. Well, there's always boarding school. Seven is too many, anyway. "Darling, this is good old fashioned cooking. It's got chicken and vegetables. You're going to love it."

After shooing away the dog and the ferret lurking under the table—she'd have to get the number for the SPCA once she moved in—Veronica dished out a serving for everyone, and while the kids pushed around the peas and stabbed a carrot or two, Shawna shrugged and took a big bite. She chewed a bit then nodded. "Not bad. I'm impressed."

Veronica smiled at Jeremy. "I haven't had the chance to do cooking like this for a family."

Shawna pointed her fork at her. "Right, because we had a chef when you were married to my dad. You were very good at ordering out, though."

Veronica gripped the edge of the table.

"Circumstances were different then. And your father liked ordering out."

"He was hardly ever home for dinner."

Veronica took a deep breath. "Well, I think my maternal instincts are finally kicking in. Maybe it just required the right child," she said through a tight smile.

"Maybe it's because you were so young back then."

Veronica stood up, smoothing down her dress. "Who wants apple pie?"

She sliced up enough servings for everyone, and gave the first one to Shaw. "You like apple, don't you?"

Shaw grabbed the plate and stared at her. "I do."

The kids poked at their pie, picking off the fresh slices on top that had gone brown since she'd cut them, but Shaw ate the whole thing.

The kids pushed away from the table. "Can we be excused?" Jenny asked.

"Yes, but thank Veronica for a nice meal," Jeremy said.

"Thank you," they said together in a way that did not sound grateful at all.

"I'll get them started on baths. You've all got school tomorrow," Shaw said.

"Aww!" they protested, as they followed her out of the room.

Good. Time for the kill. Veronica looked at Jeremy. "No pie for you?" She raised an eyebrow. "Or did you want something else for dessert, perhaps?"

"No, no. I'm full. It was good."

Oh, he's so thick. She shrugged. "I'm multi-talented. In the kitchen, and other rooms in the house." She placed her hand on his knee.

He removed it and cleared his throat. "About that.

153

Veronica, I'm sorry if I've given you the wrong impression. I've been too shocked with grief to really see what's going on around me. I thought you were here just as a friend to Dina, but I'm sensing you were hoping for something more?"

Despite the sinking feeling in her stomach, she smiled at him. "I did come here as a friend. But I've developed feelings for you, Jeremy. We'd make a wonderful team, and I love your children." *Clearly, we'd need to get a new nanny…*

He sighed. "I hope I didn't mislead you in any way. I just don't feel that way about you, Veronica. I hope we can still be friends."

She crossed her arms in a huff. "It's Shawna, isn't it?"

"I do have feelings for her. But you and I just weren't meant to be."

We'll just see about that. "You're still raw from Dina's death. Give it some time. You'll see we're perfect for each other."

"I don't think you should come over quite as often."

She looked up at him. "Of course. If that's what you want. But you can call me anytime if you change your mind."

Remarkably, she waited until she got outside to cry. She'd been able to land any man she'd ever set her sights on. How had this gone wrong?

Shawna. She'd pay. She didn't know how, but she would.

Without enough money in her wallet for a subway ride, Veronica started the long walk home. She paused in front of a bakery looking to hire. *The Naughty or Nice Bakery? Sounds perfect for me.* She jotted down the number.

She had enjoyed cooking that evening. Maybe she could even land her own cooking show someday, or her own line of celebrity cooking ware. Or she'd marry a celebrity chef! She twirled on the sidewalk, enchanted by the endless possibilities. Maybe it was time to try the working world again until she found another suitable husband.

Or until Jeremy came to his senses.

***

Shaw got the kids into bed, and Jeremy went from room to room with hugs and kisses goodnight.

"Snow, we want kisses, too!" Jake called.

She looked at Jeremy who nodded for her to go ahead. She gave them each a kiss on the head and wondered if she'd ever be lucky enough to call these children her own some day. It was remarkable, really. She'd told herself she wouldn't even think about children until she was well into her thirties, hopefully after she'd been on a few touring productions.

She followed Jeremy into the living room and they collapsed on the couch. "Dinner wasn't bad, huh? Although the apple pie tasted a bit funny." She rubbed her stomach.

"Glad I didn't have any. I don't think we'll be seeing much more of Veronica."

"Oh?"

"I told her I didn't have feelings for her. But that I did have feelings for you."

He reached for her hand and she ignored the painful twist in her stomach as he leaned over to kiss her.

***

She replayed their kiss most of the next day. She was chasing the triplets with their sneakers for a walk after day care, when her cell rang.

155

"I'm looking for Shawna White. This is the director from King productions."

Did Veronica think she was stupid? Shawna was no fool. "Very funny," she said. "Are you friends with Veronica Midas?"

"I'm sorry, did I get the wrong number? I'm trying to reach Shawna White? She tried out for our musical, and we'd like to offer her a spot."

She nearly dropped the phone; she did try out for that touring production.

Fifteen minutes later she sat down on the couch, stunned. Jeremy walked out of his office and did a double take. "Are you alright?"

She could only nod.

"What's wrong?"

"Well, nothing. It's great actually. I got the part in a musical as understudy. Their first choice broke her leg in a car accident. They want to start touring in two weeks." She stood up and started pacing.

"How long will you be gone?"

"I don't know. I don't know if I'm taking it."

He stood up and took her in his arms. "Of course you have to take it. The kids and I will still be here. This is your dream. I can't stand in the way of it."

"I don't know. I just don't know." Then she clenched her hand to her stomach, pushed away from him and rushed to the bathroom.

Where she stayed for several hours.

"Can I get you anything?" Jeremy asked outside the door.

"Can you help me get to bed?"

He opened the door, and his face looked panicked. "You're really sick."

She looked up from the cold tile floor and nodded. He lifted her in his arms and carried her to bed. He lay her down and covered her up. "Thanks, I'm freezing."

He felt her forehead. "But you're burning up. There's a doctor who lives in the building. I'm calling him. He's made house calls for the kids before."

She tried to nod, but it hurt to move her head. She couldn't remember ever being this sick.

***

The doctor looked at the thermometer. "You've got a temperature of 103. With the vomiting and ... other problems," as he discreetly put it, "I think we've got a case of food poisoning here, especially how it just suddenly hit you. What have you eaten?"

"She had chicken pot pie and apple pie last night," Jeremy said.

The doctor raised an eyebrow. "Chicken? If it wasn't cooked properly, it could be salmonella."

"Veronica cut up the apples and the chicken with a big knife and she was saying bad words. I don't think she was doing it properly," Lizzie informed them.

"The same knife? For the chicken and the apples?" Lizzie nodded.

"There's your likely answer."

"Your stepmother poisoned you?"

"Not on purpose," Shaw whispered. Or was it?

"Is Snow going to die like Mommy did?" John asked, tears welling in his eyes.

And that's the last thing Shaw heard before she fell asleep.

***

Shaw woke to the feel of soft lips against hers. Her eyes fluttered open and she saw Jeremy standing over her.

157

Surrounded by the kids, with stunned looks on their faces. "It worked! Daddy kissed her and she woke up! Daddy kissed Snow White!" one of them whispered.

Jeremy was leaning over her, smiling. "That's because I like Snow very much."

Shaw sat up, grinning at their funny nickname for her. She rubbed her eyes. "Wow, everyone is here." The kids were surrounded by the animals, all watching her.

"We were worried. You've been asleep for sixteen hours."

"I have?"

"Are you feeling better?"

She nodded.

"Then you better call King Productions because they need an answer about the tour. I told the kids you might be leaving us. They understand."

But one look at their frowns told her they did not understand at all.

Neither did she. She slumped back in bed and closed her eyes. She thought she'd always wanted a spot in a production more than anything. But now, she didn't know what she wanted. She opened her eyes and saw seven sweet little faces staring at her; and one seriously handsome face, etched with concern. And that's when she knew what she wanted. She shook her head. "I'm not going. We've still got to learn how to whistle *The Star Spangled Banner*. Or do the bunny hop. I promised, and I don't go back on my promises."

The kids jumped up and clapped and danced around the room while Jeremy kissed her again. Then his phone rang and he answered it. "Veronica? No. We definitely don't want any cookies. Shaw's been very sick from the meal you made Sunday. Lizzie said you used the same knife on the chicken and the apples?" He paused for a moment. "Well, I seriously suggest you taking a food safety course before taking a job at any bakery. Good luck, Veronica. I wish you the best."

"Did she purposely try to kill me?" Shaw asked, only half kidding.

"No, but it might have been a deep dark wish. She knows there's no future with me. She knows I love you."

"And so do we, Snow!" said Jenny, as the seven children, two cats, dog, birds and ferret piled onto her bed.

"Just promise you won't be a bad stepmother like Veronica's been to you," Maddy said.

Shaw laughed. "I think you're getting ahead of yourselves."

But Jeremy raised an eyebrow in a way that suggested they knew exactly how things would play out. And it would be the role of a lifetime.

"Goldie"
by Lisa Scott

Goldie Lockston counted the children that danced past her in a conga line led by a woman in a rabbit costume and sent up a silent prayer of thanks that she was in charge of one dog for the week instead of seven energetic children. Yikes. Goldie wasn't the biggest dog lover in the world, but at least she had a place to stay for a few days.

It's not that Goldie was homeless; she was more than welcome to live with her parents. That's where her bills went. That's where her cello from seventh grade was stored, and homeless people certainly did not own cellos. Technically, on job applications and census forms she listed her parents' address as her permanent address. But she couldn't live there. Her mother still hounded her to get a real job instead of chasing her 'silly art dream.' And to 'stick to a curfew if you're living under my roof, young lady.' Plus, there wasn't a very big art scene in her hometown unless the paint-your-own-pottery store counted. Which it did not. Living at home at age twenty-five just wasn't an option.

So, she and her pink luggage set moved from place to place when friends had the room to spare. It's not like she was sleeping in cars or under bridges. *That* was homeless. And she hated the word 'squatter.' It made her think of the time she'd peed in the woods during her family's camping trip in the mountains. She'd been terrified a bear would grab her the entire time.

No, squatter wasn't the right word either. Serial houseguest? Mobile tenant? One thing was sure, she'd learned how to pack light: one suitcase for her clothes, one for her art supplies. Her purse was stuffed with essentials like makeup, travel-sized toothpaste, and mouthwash. It was a fine setup.

She fingered the key in her hand and tightened the grip on her luggage. This particular arrangement was riskier than usual, but who'd ever find out? Aurora had been desperate for someone to fill in for her pet-sitting service, and Goldie needed a break from the oh-my-god-yes-yes-more passion fest unfolding in her friend Ariel's apartment. Luckily, the guy who lived here had told the doorman at Grimm Towers to expect a pet sitter to stop by, so she'd had no trouble getting in the building.

She took a deep breath and opened the door to the apartment. She rolled her eyes as she walked into the grand marble foyer. *People really live like this?* Setting down her suitcases, she took in the giant crystal chandelier and marble columns. The mortgage on this place for a month could probably keep her living comfortably for a year. *Some people truly live in a different world,* she thought.

A high-pitched whine from the other end of the apartment caught her attention. That must be Miss Sniggles, her charge for the week. Aurora told her Miss Sniggles had to be fed twice daily and let out every four hours. She hadn't exactly asked Goldie to stay overnight to complete the job. But it was the perfect way to escape the love nest taking over Ariel's apartment. Besides, Aurora was spending the weekend with her guy upstate. She'd never find out. And really, it was almost like a bonus service. It was round-the-clock dog sitting. Some people would get premium pay for this, and all she was doing was crashing for a few days. She nodded to herself, pleased with her generous spirit.

Kicking off her shoes, she slid across the marble floor, ala Tom Cruise in *Risky Business*. Sure, this was kind of risky, but she'd be out of here before next Saturday at five when the owner was due back. Usually, people knew when she was crashing at their place. This was the first time she was, technically, an uninvited guest. She wrinkled her nose at the phrase. It made her sound like a roach, or something to be caught in a trap.

She followed the sound of the whimpering dog and pushed open a door at the end of the hall. That's right, she'd forgotten. Aurora had told her the dog had its own room. *Its own room.* And this dog was small enough that a shoebox would have sufficed for a doghouse. A teacup Chihuahua? Is that what Aurora had called it? And it was lounging on a miniature canopy bed. For the first time in her life, she'd met a dog that had it better than her. She was glad she wouldn't be meeting the man who lived here; she might be tempted to lecture him on the foolishness of excess.

But still, the tiny dog prancing at her feet was adorable. It couldn't help that it was a pampered plaything for some rich guy. She picked up the pooch and the little thing fit in her hand. "You are such a cutie!" She'd been expecting something big like a German shepherd, not a stuffed animal come to life. A crystal-studded dog leash hung from a peg on the wall, along with itty-bitty coats and clothes for the dog. She read the name engraved on the dog tag. "Miss Sniggles? Oh, you poor thing." She patted the dog's head then set her down, trying to imagine what kind of guy owned a pet like this.

The dog trotted after her as she inspected the apartment, its little claws tapping on the floor. One thing was for sure, Goldie needed coffee. Ariel and her boyfriend were very expressive in their lovemaking. A pillow wrapped around your head only blocks out so much of that, and now she was crabby and tired and more than a smidge jealous. It'd been a while since she'd been in a similar position. Or positions, from the sound of it last night.

Besides the dog, nothing about the apartment gave her any insight into the man who lived here. There was no exquisite art hanging on the walls, no photos. The place featured functional, quality furniture and zero clutter. The apartment looked like it'd been plucked from a designer magazine. *No soul*, she whispered to herself.

She opened a cupboard and started searching for coffee. It was a little weird going through a stranger's things. But Aurora had told her Blake Behr always said for her to help herself to anything she wanted while watching the dog. Surely, he'd extend the same courtesy to Aurora's fill-in girl. This guy must love his coffee—he had at least a dozen different kinds to choose from.

Goldie had never tried Brazilian coffee, so she ground the beans, dumped them in the gold plated filter—*Seriously?*—and waited for the caffeine kick she so desperately needed.

While the coffee brewed, she inspected the kitchen with its gleaming stainless steel appliances, expensive cookware, but very little food. These cupboards were practically empty, except for old crackers, sardines and olives.

She looked at Miss Sniggles. "I think we're ordering out, kiddo."

The coffee finished brewing and she poured herself a cup. She was the only women she knew who drank her coffee black. Fancy creams and flavorings for her brew weren't appealing. For someone who lived a fairly nomadic life, she was quite picky in her tastes.

She warmed her hands on the mug and inhaled the scent. "Nice." But she spit out the first sip. "Ugh. Too strong." She dumped the pot in the sink. Searching through the coffee choices, she picked a Columbian roast.

She made up another pot while the dog curled up in the corner and snored softly. The apartment was immaculate; she'd have to be sure to clean up after herself Saturday morning. Staying with other people usually meant you put away your stuff and tidied up immediately, but maybe this week she'd cut herself some slack and do it all at the end.

The last of the coffee dribbled through the filter, and she poured herself another cup. Taking a sip, she frowned. "Yuck. Way too weak." Maybe she wasn't destined for coffee today.

"I'll try one more time." She chose a French blend and crossed her fingers that the third time would be a charm. Miss Sniggles was awake now, dancing around Goldie's feet. "Do you have to go out?"

The dog yipped at her.

Goldie got her leash and poured herself a cup of coffee in a travel mug. She took a sip. "Perfect!" Carrying the dog was easier than following her teeny-tiny steps. They crossed the street to Sherwood Park, and Miss Sniggles immediately relieved her thimble sized bladder. Goldie let her sniff around while she inspected the park. It was a nice late-summer day, and she'd love to paint a few watercolors while she had the chance. She preferred oils, but canvases were a lot bulkier to haul around than sheets of watercolor paper. The owner of Naughty or Nice bakery had agreed to let her hold an art show there in a few weeks, and she wanted to have as many framed paintings and note cards for sale as possible.

She took Miss Sniggles back inside and carried her suitcase of supplies out to the park. A portable easel, a folding chair, and her water colors all fit inside. People were always surprised to see her unpack all that gear from her suitcase. She set up her palette and scanned the park for inspiration. On a sunny late September day, it wasn't hard to find beautiful scenarios, but she liked to capture the unexpected. Most people might be tempted by the sight of colorful trees and use their burnt umber and sienna to recreate a panoramic view of the park. Goldie always focused on the overlooked. She spotted a forgotten Frisbee nestled under the leaves and started painting that; the perfect image of a summer just passed.

Dabbing her brush in the paint and swooping it along the paper, she wondered what was next for her after this dog-sitting gig. She really should have some sort of five-year plan. That's what all the financial planning articles she'd read at Ariel's had advised. Getting by day-to-day was becoming difficult. She'd been selling her artwork online and at the occasional show. It would be a dream to do this full time and to have her own little place to live—she certainly didn't need a luxury apartment like Blake's. A simple studio would do. But even that was a stretch right now. The term starving artist had more than a thread of truth in it.

She finished two paintings, pleased with her work, and went back to the apartment. She wandered from room to room, trying out the chairs and sofas, looking for the perfect spot to curl up and read a book. She finally found the ideal recliner in a den, and kicked up the footrest. Trying to concentrate on her book, she was distracted by an unfamiliar sense of dissatisfaction. She should be thrilled with this set up—alone for a week! No distractions, no inadvertent voyeurism. She was more solo than Han.

She set down her book. But maybe that was it. She usually wasn't alone. She crashed with friends and rarely had a moment to herself. Perhaps being alone was lonelier than she liked. Some friends subtly suggested she find a boyfriend to shack up with. But she would not start dating a guy just in the hopes of finding a place to live. And dating while you're bouncing from place to place isn't the easiest thing to do.

It was time to let Miss Sniggles out again, and Goldie walked a few blocks to grab a slice of pizza and a salad. She made herself a setting at the huge dining room table to enjoy her feast, but it only made her feel lonely again.

When it was time for bed, she inspected the three bedrooms. She assumed the biggest one with the silky, chocolate-brown duvet was the master suite. She'd feel a little odd sleeping in his room, so she checked out what she assumed were the guest bedrooms. Deciding on a cream-colored room with an antique sleigh bed and quilt, she hauled in her suitcase. She cleaned up, slipped into her nightgown, and crawled under the covers. Miss Sniggles must have been feeling lonely too, because she left her own luxurious room and wandered into Goldie's. The dog stood at the side of the bed and whined.

Goldie patted the edge of the bed, encouraging her to jump up. Then she realized an itty-bitty pooch wouldn't be able to make a leap like that, so she picked her up, and the dog snuggled next to her on the pillow.

Goldie sunk into the mattress. It was nice at first, but then she felt uncomfortable, constantly changing positions, punching her pillow and causing Miss Sniggles to growl softly at her. Sighing, she got up, scooped the dog into her arms and went to the next room down the hall. She peeled back the covers, set the dog next to her and tried to find her "spot." After a few tosses and turns, she stared at the ceiling. Why couldn't she get comfortable in this home? Was she feeling guilty about crashing here? Was she uncomfortable staying in such luxurious digs? Whatever the reason, the bed was so hard she couldn't stand it another minute.

Scooping up a disgruntled Miss Sniggles one more time, she stood in the doorway of the master bedroom. Certainly, the man of the house had a comfortable bed. And she was desperate for sleep. She'd wash the sheets before she left. Setting the dog down again, she crawled under the covers, set her head on the pillow and sighed. "This is perfect." And she fell right asleep.

***

Blake couldn't decide if he was more annoyed or relieved that the cruise with his parents had been cancelled. The cruise line had offered to book them onto another cruise leaving the next day, but once his mother had heard the words "Norovirus" and "outbreak" her cruising days were over. Traveling with them was never easy, but what a waste the last two days had been. His mother was disappointed, his father was angry, and now Blake had to find them a new twenty-fifth wedding anniversary present. Someone owed him big time in the karma department.

While his parents walked down the street to grab a

bite to eat from the all night deli, he brought their luggage upstairs, dropping it in his front hall. Something in the kitchen immediately caught his attention. Dirty dishes in the sink? Did Aurora make herself something to eat while she was here?

He walked through the apartment. Someone had left a reading light on in his den. The doors to the guest bedrooms were open. And why wasn't that darn dog running out of her room to greet him? Miss Sniggles was annoying, but she was always happy to see him, perhaps the only creature that felt that way these days.

He flipped on the hall light and paused outside his room. *What the hell?* Someone was sleeping in his bed, and he didn't recognize the tangle of blond curls as Aurora's. He walked into his room, planted his fists and his hips and cleared his throat. "Hope my bed is comfortable."

The girl sucked in a breath and sat up, her eyes wide with panic. "Blake? What are you doing home so early?" She pressed her hand against her chest, covering up her low cut nightgown.

He raised an eyebrow. "How do you know me, but I don't know you?"

She blinked and gulped. "I'm Goldie Lockston, Aurora's friend. She had to go out of town on an emergency. She asked if I could take care of the dog."

"She didn't have permission to stay here."

Her mouth opened and closed, and if he weren't annoyed with her he would have thought she was sexy, in a disheveled way. Miss Sniggles looked at him and curled up next to the girl, the furry little traitor.

Goldie's shoulders slumped. "I'm sorry. I kind of had nowhere to stay, so I crashed here while I was watching the dog. It's almost like an extra service, really. Round the clock dog sitting." She smiled at him hopefully.

"It's more like a bonus, free room and board."

Out came a scowl. "I'll get my stuff together."

Surprisingly, he didn't want to see her go. In fact, she might be able to help him out. He held up a hand. "Hang on a minute. I won't fire Aurora and I won't call police on you if you do one thing for me."

She narrowed her eyes. "What?"

He exhaled. This was going to sound bad. "My parents are on their way up any minute, and I want them to think you're my girlfriend."

She blinked at him. "Why?"

He ran his hand through his hair. "Because my mother has been on a matchmaking rampage since I broke up with my girlfriend six months ago. In an effort to put an end to her constant suggestions and inquires, I might have told her I've been seeing someone."

"Ahh. And that's who I'm pretending to be."

He nodded.

"But I'd never go out with someone like you."

He cocked his head. "Oh really? And how do you know that?"

"From a quick glance around your apartment. It looks like it was staged."

"Yes, I bought it that way in case I ever have to move. It's ready to sell."

"But how can you live here if you're ready to leave at a moment's notice?"

He opened his mouth, ready to argue, but what was the point? "They won't be here long. It hardly matters if you'd really date me or not."

She shrugged. "Fine. If I agree, will you let me stay here the rest of the week until I figure out where to go next?"

His eyebrows shot up. "You're homeless?"

"Not exactly." She yawned and stretched. "Well, kind of, I guess." She sighed. "Yes. For now, I am without a home, so I'll play along. So, who am I? What do I do?"

He looked up at the ceiling. He was placing his future in the hands of a homeless apartment crasher who thought she was too good to date him? "I have a feeling I'm going to regret this, but here goes. My parents will be up here any minute. You're Nicole Dawson, you're a lawyer on track to make partner, and we've been dating for three months."

She shook her head. "No way. I'm not lawyer material at all."

He sucked in a breath and counted to five. "Yes, you are. I told them my girlfriend was a lawyer."

Chewing on her bottom lip, she squinted her eyes, then pointed at him. "How about this. I was a lawyer, but I'm thinking about quitting to pursue my love of art. Which is true. I'm an artist."

"Which is why you're homeless."

She nodded. "And, it can lead to the perfect scenario for a breakup. You can't believe I'd do something so irresponsible. You can't spend the rest of your life with someone who makes rash decisions like quitting their job to pursue their passion."

"Or crashing in a stranger's apartment."

"Well, that too. But that's not part of our story, here." She tucked her legs underneath her, enthusiastically creating their tale. "Okay, now your turn.

I know your name is Blake, your apartment is so generically decorated I wasn't sure someone actually lived here and for some reason you have a pet dog more suitable for an eight-year-old girl than a hot thirty-something guy."

That caught his attention and he hesitated for a moment. She thought he was hot. He suppressed a smile. Hot—not rich, or a good catch, or a suitable mate. All the things he usually heard from the women who ran in his circle. *Hot*. His insides hummed. And then he remembered his emasculating pet blinking up at him; and that Goldie wasn't interested in him. "The dog was a gift to my ex, and she refused to take it because it reminded her of me." He rolled his eyes. "I don't have the heart to give her away. And I hired someone specifically to make my apartment look neutral not generic. What else?"

"What do you do for a living?"

"I'm a lawyer close to making partner."

"Do we get along? Do you love me like mad?" She clasped her hands in front of her in a romantic gesture.

"Excuse me?"

She shrugged. "Am I a casual girlfriend or is this serious? What did you get me for Christmas? Which side of the bed do I sleep on? What have you told your parents about me? Will they be surprised I'm here?"

Right. That was a little strange. "I'll tell them the dog sitter bailed on me—that part is true—and that you, my lovely Nicole, came to watch my dog. They shouldn't be here long. We'll only have to keep up this ruse for half an hour or so."

"I've had shorter relationships."

He raised an eyebrow.

"Kidding. It just feels like that sometimes."

He heard his parents come through the front door. "Can you put on a robe or something?" He gestured to her short, silky pink gown.

"I travel light. No room for a robe. Got one you can lend me?"

He pulled his plush white robe out of his closet and handed it to her.

Hopping off the bed, she tugged her arms through the sleeves. "Are we breaking up right now?"

"No, just say hello and I'll give them the bad news later this week that it's over."

"But then she'll just try to set you up with someone else."

He shook his head. "I'll be so devastated I won't be able to date anyone for a long, long time."

She nodded in agreement. "It's true. You would be devastated if I dumped you. Most guys are."

He laughed. "Okay, Nicole. Time to meet the parents."

***

Goldie checked her spring of blond curls in the mirror and took a deep breath. *This is what you get for crashing at a stranger's.* Maybe it was time to buckle down and get a real job. She shuddered at the thought.

She followed Blake into the kitchen and figured the less she said the better. His mother and father were arguing over whether or not to pick up milk and bread on the way home. They stopped bickering and looked up when she and Blake walked into the kitchen.

"Oh, hello there," his mother said. She blinked rapidly under shiny black bangs. She was a beautiful woman, with green eyes just like Blake.

"Who's this, son?" his father asked. He was tall and

172

lean like Blake. It was like Blake had taken their best qualities to become their super hottie son. Super-hottie-without-a-sense-of-humor-or-creative-decorating-taste son.

Blake stood behind Goldie and put his hands on her shoulders. "Mom, Dad, this is Nicole. Turns out my dog sitter had to cancel and contacted Nicole, so she came over to watch Miss Sniggles."

"I just love that little thing," Goldie said.

"You do know that was his ex's dog, right?" Mrs. Behr asked.

Goldie nodded. "But it's not like I'm wearing her old shoes or engagement ring or something. It's just a cute little doggie!" On cue, Miss Sniggles came bounding into the room, pawing on Goldie's leg to be picked up.

"So, Blake tells us you're a lawyer," his father said.

She paused. Now wasn't the time to announce the news of her sudden career change. "I am. I'm not so sure it's my calling, though." She tried her best to sound wistful.

Mrs. Behr looked alarmed. "Why not?"

She shrugged. What are all the reasons she'd hate being a lawyer? "Well, the wardrobe for one. All those stuffy suits?" She made a face. "And people are constantly telling me stupid lawyer jokes. And then dealing with all those murders and thieves?" She threw up hands up in the air as if to say, 'What can you do?'

Mrs. Behr held a finger in the air, as if requesting to ask a question. "I thought you were a real estate lawyer."

Blake cleared his throat. "Oh, she is. She helps the murderers and thieves find housing when they leave jail."

"There are lawyers for that?" his mother asked.

Goldie nodded. "Blake thinks it's a good career path

for me."

He rubbed her arm. "Well, now that you've said hello, why don't you go back to bed, darling? You must be tired and not up for much more talking," he said through a tight smile.

"Yes, go back to sleep, Nicole. I'm so sorry we woke you. We can chat in the morning." His mother turned to Blake. "I've decided we're going to stay here tonight since your father doesn't want to stop at the grocery store for milk."

"We can get it in the morning," his dad grumbled, crossing his arms.

Blake froze. "Stay here? Really? I thought you were anxious to get home? I thought you were just stopping in for a moment?" He probably didn't realize his grip on her arm had tightened. A lot.

"That was before I knew we'd have a chance to get to know Nicole. We won't be in the way. Not a bit. We'll take the guest room down the hall and see you in the morning. Now you two run off. I'm sure you're eager for some time alone."

Goldie waggled her eyebrows. "Oh, we are."

His mother forced a smile. "We'll see you in the morning. So nice to meet you."

"You, too." Goldie walked out of the kitchen back to Blake's bedroom, where he closed the door behind him.

He looked up at the ceiling, shaking his head. "A real estate attorney for criminals. Quite a niche market."

"You didn't tell me what kind of lawyer. I had to wing it." She took off the robe. "So, what do we do now?"

"You can sleep in the bed. I'll take the couch."

"Thanks!" She hopped on the bed, then started

bouncing on it, causing it to creak. "This way they'll think you really missed me. That'll make the break up that more dramatic." She stood up and jumped, kicking her legs up behind her.

Creak, creak, creak.

"Stop it!" he hissed.

She stopped bouncing and sat down with a huff. "You know, I think if I had an actual relationship with you, it really would last only an hour or so."

He rolled his eyes. "God willing."

***

The bed that had seemed so comfortable was now offering Goldie no sleep, not with Blake and tossing and turning on the couch. She imagined his muscles flexing under his t-shirt. Sure, he was grumpy and uptight and lived in an ostentatious apartment, but there was something intriguing and attractive about him.

And of course, she was busy wondering where she'd go next. One week here would give her a chance to regroup. Maybe it was time to settle for a real job. Something that would give her the means to find her own place. For the first time, she wanted to stay put. Something about Blake's place grounded her, made her long for stability.

The next morning, she'd hit the want ads. She would.

That decision must have settled her, because she found herself waking to a sunny room and the smell of coffee. Blake was gone, and she hoped his parents weren't up yet so she had a moment to talk to Blake and get their story straight.

Grabbing his robe—and inhaling the faint masculine scent that lingered in the fabric of the collar—she

175

wandered to the kitchen. His parents were there, chatting with Blake. His mother looked up and smiled when Goldie stepped in the room. "Good morning, dear. Wait until you hear the good news."

"You're leaving for another cruise? Right now?" she asked.

"Oh, no. My days at sea are over after that debacle. No, I was just telling Blake I got an email from a friend inviting us up to their cottage in the mountains for a few days. Since we all had plans to be on vacation anyway, we should go. It'll give us a chance to get to know each other better."

Goldie's heart quickened. She was torn. This act was going to be tough to pull off. But a few days in the mountains? She could get some incredible painting done there, and have plenty of work for her show.

Then she thought about squatting in the woods all those years ago and the possibility of bears. "There's indoor plumbing, right?"

"Of course."

Before Goldie could say yes, Blake fixed her with a stare. "I told my mother you have that thing to do this week. At that place."

But she'd already fallen in love with the idea of a painting trip to the mountains. A free painting trip to the mountains, and another few days of accommodations. She waved him off. "Oh, that thing? No, didn't I tell you? That's been cancelled. While you were away. Cancelled!" she said, like it was the best news ever.

He gave her a tight smile and exhaled slowly.

His mother clapped her hands together. "Excellent. Then it's settled. We'll leave this morning." She shrugged. "We're already packed."

"Can I talk to you for a minute, Nicole?" Blake asked.

She followed him into the other room, Miss Sniggles trailing after them. "What do you think you're doing?"

She'd thought of the same question and she was a step ahead of him. "Setting the stage for the breakup. I'm going to bring my art supplies, do some painting, and that'll lend credibility to our breakup story." Goldie shrugged like she'd been explaining the ABC's to a kindergartener for the tenth time.

He closed his eyes and rubbed the back of his neck. "I've got a really bad feeling about this."

"It's fine. What could go wrong?"

***

Goldie stroked the poor pooch in her lap. "How could you not know she gets car sick?"

"I don't usually bring her with me in the car."

"She's a purse pooch. They're made to be portable." The dog barfed up another tablespoon of vomit, and Goldie cleaned it up with the last napkin from the glove compartment.

"And how did you happen to name her Miss Sniggles?"

Blake sighed. "My ex thought it sounded like a mix between giggle and snuggles."

Goldie stared at him for a moment. "For real?"

He could barely manage a nod.

"Huh. Did you meet her when you were in a coma? Was it like that movie where Sandra Bullock showed up and pretended to be the guy's girlfriend? Because that doesn't strike me as your type." Miss Sniggles burped.

"Is she going to be okay?" Blake asked.

177

Goldie smiled at him. "Aww, you really love her don't you?"

"More than he loved Katrina, apparently," his mother said.

Blake grumbled something and looked out the window.

"One thing's for sure, that dog loves you, Nicole," his mother said, leaning forward between the seats. "It's like she's forgotten all about Katrina." His mother sniffed, and his father patted her hand. "I'm sorry. I thought she was the one. I even had the reception venue all picked out." She straightened her shoulders and forced a brave smile. "But now you're here, and I swear, I feel an instant connection with you, Nicole. I've got a very good feeling about this."

"Oh, me, too." Goldie turned around and squeezed her hand.

Coming to a stop at a red light, Blake cleared his throat. "I don't place much stock in 'feelings'." He made air quotes around the word.

His father leaned forward. "Son, I had feeling your mother would be the one the moment I saw her."

"Aww, that's so sweet," Goldie said. "I can tell you two are still really close. It's lovely."

They beamed at each other in the back seat and the dog threw up again.

"Exactly how I feel, Miss Sniggles." Blake shot Goldie a look as the light turned green.

Fine, fine, she got the point. Time to set the stage for the breakup. "So, I'm going to be spending some time myself painting. Hope that's okay with everyone."

"Painting?" his mother asked, sitting up straight. "You're a painter?"

Here we go, Goldie thought, mentally rubbing her

hands.

"Yes. It's my true passion. Blake thinks its silly."

"Silly? I was an art major for a time in college, until my father told me to be more practical and get my teaching degree." She sighed. "I married your father and never used it."

"What?" asked Blake. "I never heard that."

"I didn't want you to think badly of your grandfather. A person should never stand in the way of someone's dream." His mother nodded emphatically.

Blake gripped the steering wheel. "When I told you I wanted to be a writer and major in English, you guys insisted I go pre-law instead."

His mother looked out the window. "Well, that's different. No one can support themselves as a writer. You'd never have the apartment you have if you'd become a writer." Mrs. Behr's voice trailed off.

Goldie nodded. "I quit the cello back in high school and have regretted it ever since. It's still at my mother's house. Who knows? Maybe I could've been a concert cellist."

Everyone was quiet.

"But it's never too late, Blake," Goldie said. "You could write as a hobby, like I do with my art." Goldie nodded at him, then turned around and looked at his mother. "And you could borrow my art supplies when we get up there and give it a go."

"Really?" His mother's voice was so hopeful it hurt.

Blake bounced his head on the back of the seat.

Goldie smiled back at her. "Of course. I'm working in watercolors."

His mother sucked in a breath. "My favorite. I'm so glad our cruise was cancelled. This is going to be much more fun than Bermuda."

***

Blake carried in Goldie's luggage—presumably everything she had in the world—and wondered how he was going to survive this weekend.

A mouse scurried across the floor and he swore. "We'll need to get some traps."

"Is that how you treat surprise guests who are hungry?" Goldie scolded.

He fixed her with a stare. "Ones that eat my food without asking, yes."

"Sometimes unexpected houseguests are helpful Blake, don't forget that. Now let's just shoo this little guy outside." She grabbed a broom leaning against the wall and chased the mouse outside.

With his hands on his hips he shook his head. How could someone so frustrating also be so appealing? She was unlike any woman he'd ever gone out with before. Any other woman would've been halfway to the hardware store by now buying mousetraps. Or standing on the table, screaming. No, Goldie was finding the rodent alternative housing.

He tried to pretend he wasn't put out that Miss Sniggles was following Goldie everywhere, like she was the one providing the furnished room and designer doggie bed and organic dog food, the ungrateful little thing, not unlike her previous owner, Katrina. Blake hadn't had the best luck with women, female or canine.

"I'm going to take a dip in the lake, care to join me?" she asked Blake. It was an unseasonably warm day; one last blast of summer.

His mother hated swimming, so that would give them plenty of time alone so he could get this damn thing

180

back on track. Goldie was being way too cute and personable. "Sure, I'll get changed and meet you down there."

He marched down to the beach, a towel wrapped around his shoulder, determined to get her out of here. He was composing the speech in his head as he spotted her splashing along the shore of the lake with three little children. Shocking, she'd made new friends already. She was probably getting their addresses so she could stay for a visit. But he couldn't help smile as he watched her. He had to admit, part of the reason he was so annoyed with her was because she was everything he wished he were: spontaneous, carefree, friendly.

No, Blake was all about schedules, priorities, and plans. He'd been voted Most Serious in high school and had taken it as a great badge of honor instead of the snub that it was meant to be. They'd actually created the category for him.

He didn't have an answer for that. He blew out a deep breath. This breakup was going to be hard on them all. Might as well enjoy the relationship while it lasted. He waved to her and she waved back, all smiles and radiant beauty. No wonder Miss Sniggles and his mother liked her. Who wouldn't?

She kicked up a spray of water as he walked down to her. "Belly-flop contest? You in?" She gestured to the floating dock a little ways from shore.

He was about to launch into all the reasons he wouldn't be doing *that*, when she pulled him by the hand and splashed into the water. And damn, if he didn't squeeze her hand back.

***

His stomach was still stinging from the smack of water on abs during their belly flop contest. Despite her much smaller frame, she'd somehow managed to produce a bigger splash than he did, and all the kids along the shore named her the belly-flop queen of the world.

"So you're the belly-flopping queen? I must get you a crown." He scooped her up and ran into the water with her, tossing her into the lake as she shrieked in protest. She came up out of the water and sloshed back to him, and he tried his best to ignore the glistening beads of water, cascading down her cleavage, lucky droplets.

Then she reached up, lacing her hands behind his neck and pulling him in for a kiss. Despite the warm day, she shivered in his arms as she pressed her lips against his, and he pulled her closer, keeping her wonderful mouth against his a bit longer. He didn't know what had brought on her sudden passion, but he wasn't arguing.

Finally, he pulled back, looking at her face for a reaction. *Did the kiss feel as good to her, too?*

She shrugged. "Just wanted to make it really convincing for your parents." She gestured to his mom and dad standing on the shore, waving.

His heart sank. "Right, right. Of course." He cleared his throat. "Good call."

His parents leaned into each other, watching them. They'd never forgive him for breaking up with her. And he'd never forgive himself if he fell for her. He had to be careful.

Easier said than done.

***

After they got dried off and had lunch, Goldie gathered up the painting supplies.

His mother patted his shoulder as he sat at the kitchen table trying not to watch Goldie's luscious lips closing over a strawberry. "Come watch us, darling. You've never seen your mother in action."

Yikes, that was one way to cool off his lustful thoughts.

After that hot, wet kiss in the lake, Blake was thinking it'd be best to put some space between him and Goldie. Watching her paint—imagining what else her

182

fingers could do besides grip a brush—was probably a bad idea, but his mother looked more excited than the time he got her tickets to the Jiminy Shoes trunk show, so how could he say no?

And Goldie looked pretty pleased, too.

***

Goldie's hand shook as she focused on the tree trunk growing up around a big rock. It's not that she wasn't used to an audience; people often stopped to watch her work when she was set up in the park. She just wasn't used to the gaze of a hot man who made her hands tremble while he watched. Oh, and his mother and father. Zero pressure to perform.

"That's simply gorgeous," his mother said. "I'd been wondering which angle of the mountain I was going to paint, and you found this interesting detail to focus on and it really captures the feeling so much more." She shook her head. "Do you sell your work?"

"I try. I have shows here and there."

"I'd love to host an exhibition at my friend's gallery. Perhaps we can both put out a few pieces. Maybe right before the holidays?"

Goldie's gut twisted. She wouldn't be with Blake for the holidays. But why spoil the mood? "Sure, that would be wonderful."

Blake's mother focused on a patch of moss instead of the mountain vista, while Blake and his father flicked on a radio and listened to a football game. She blinked back tears that threatened to spill, realizing how perfect this all felt; and perfectly fake at the same time. Of course his mother was enchanted with her; she thought she was a lawyer and an artist, not someone who would *need* a lawyer to represent her when charged with staying in someone's home uninvited. She could imagine the disappointment on her face if she found out.

It would probably look quite similar to the look her mother gave her every time she came home without news of a job or a new boyfriend her mother could pin her hopes on.

With their painting gear packed up, plans were made for dinner. They laughed and joked through a delicious meal at a fancy restaurant, trying its hardest to look like a casual old log cabin instead of a place that served thirty dollar pasta entrees. She could feed herself for a week with pasta from the grocery store for thirty dollars. She kept forgetting in real life, they were from totally different worlds.

But his parents had no clue. "I don't know how you've gotten our son to lighten up, but you're good for him, Nicole. I haven't seen him smile like this in a long time," Mrs. Behr said.

"I think I can figure out how she manages," his father said.

"Ted!" His mom tried to seem horrified, but fought back a grin and playfully slapped her husband's arm.

Goldie looked down and knew she was blushing. "I think he just works too hard. This vacation was a nice break for him. All work and no play makes Blake a dull boy, right?"

"Wow, Katrina was always after you to work more so you'd make partner sooner," his mom said.

"Life's more than work." Goldie shrugged.

"You don't want to let this one get away, son." His father winked at him.

Goldie ached inside realizing how nice it would feel if their words were true. She wasn't anyone's catch. An apartment-hopping, jobless artist? His parents would drive her right back to the city if they knew.

With that thought, she wanted more. She was done wandering, hoping she'd find what was right for her. This was right.

Too bad what she was doing was totally wrong.

***

After dinner, his parents dropped them off at the cottage and claimed they were going out for a drink. He doubted they'd be dropping by the local saloon; there weren't too many martini bars in this neck of the woods.

Miss Sniggles yipped and danced at their heels as they returned. Goldie scooped her up. "Did you miss us?" Goldie asked, nuzzling her nose in the scruff of the dog's fur.

"Seriously, she likes you better than Katrina."

"Sounds like she was a winner."

Blake laughed. "One of my many mistakes." Would he be making another with Goldie?

"So, your parents probably think we're up to no good here all alone," she said, in a soft hopeful voice. Blake was the first to admit he could be a dolt when it came to women, but he knew desire when he heard it.

Which is why he took her head in his hands, and walked her back against the wall, kissing her like he was about to move to Antarctica. Because really, who knew if he'd ever get the chance to do this again?

She plopped the dog on the floor and kissed him back. "What was that for," she asked, breathless. "I doubt your parents are peeking through the windows."

He shrugged. "The fresh mountain air is making me crazy, I guess."

What *had* he been thinking? Was he really interested in this nomadic artist, or was this just his subconscious saying, *"Score! It's a freebie pass for a little fun without the guilt when it's over."*

Either way, it was more than he could handle tonight. He couldn't be falling for this woman. He stepped back from her. "I'm heading to bed. I'll see you in the morning." He walked to his room without looking back so he didn't lose his nerve.

***

"When are you going to dump me?" Goldie asked two days later, as they packed their things to return to the city. They'd spent a wonderful day hiking through the forest, and then Goldie finished a few more paintings as Blake sat and watched.

185

He folded his beach towel. "Oh, no. You're dumping me. I need to be distraught and broken hearted. My mother's so in love with you she'd hate me now if I dumped you."

She shook her head. "But I can't break up with you."

He dropped his head back. "Goldie, you're a great girl and a lot of fun, and you're an amazing kisser, but I can't have a girlfriend right now. I'm so wrapped up in my career, it's just not fair. I'm being honest."

I'm an amazing kisser? She shook the idea out of her head and put her hand on her hip, tapping her toe. "I mean, your mother wouldn't think I'd break up with you. Here's our story: you find out I'm quitting law to pursue art, and my irresponsibility makes you wild. Why would I leave you?"

He shrugged. "Because I demanded you keep your job." He pointed at her. "I was unreasonable; I didn't support you. And you got mad."

"But you've been really nice about my painting." Miss Sniggles hopped on her lap and licked her hand. "You said my paintings were unique and thought provoking." She'd almost cried when he said that the day before. She looked down, running a finger through the dog's fur. "That's the nicest thing anyone's ever said about my art."

"Nicer than your parents?"

"They think it's a waste. Just like you do. At least, that's what you're going to tell your mother." Oh, it felt horrible saying that.

He frowned. And they stopped talking about the breakup.

***

Back in the city, Blake knew he should've gone back to work. But he told himself it was smart to stay at home to keep an eye on Goldie. Maybe she was really a thief who was going to rob him blind. *Yeah, right.* But instead of going back to the office, he watched her paint at the park. They took Miss Sniggles for such long walks, they ended up having to carry her. And they explored all the restaurants he'd been meaning to try. Basically, they were acting like a couple; and he liked it.

On Friday, he was disappointed when he realized he only had three more days of vacation left. And he wasn't looking forward to going back to the office. Not just because he wouldn't be spending time with Goldie, but the endless work just didn't appeal to him.

After feeding the dog, Goldie was ready for dinner. It was ten blocks away, and normally, he would've hopped in a cab. But Goldie wanted to walk, and he looked forward to her observations as they strolled along. She noticed things he never saw: the strip of paper from a fortune cookie skittering along the street; a lonely button caught in the groove of the sidewalk; a balloon floating away in the sky.

As they ambled along the sidewalk, letting people stream around them, Goldie reached for his hand and pointed across the street. "Look, a pigeon is sitting right on top of that fire hydrant. I wish I could stop and paint it."

Then she started swinging their hands—and he didn't stop her. *Who is this man and what has he done with Blake,* he wondered.

He looked over at Goldie, grinning at the sky, and pulled her to him, kissing her right in the middle of the sidewalk.

When his hands started wandering down her back, he remembered they were in public, and stepped back.

"Wow," she said, in a husky voice. "That was unexpected. I mean you don't kiss just anybody in the middle of the sidewalk." Her eyes sparkled. "It's kind of special, isn't it?"

"Yeah, it is."

They walked in silence to the restaurant. Blake didn't know what to say about what was happening between them. He didn't know if it was real, or the result of their ruse.

They ordered champagne at dinner to celebrate her art show at the bakery the next day, but neither one talked about what was going to happen Monday when he went back to work. They hadn't talked about their impending break up in a few days.

**

The next morning, Goldie had eaten more passion bread at the Naughty and Nice bakery than she cared to admit, but so far, she'd made zero sales. The bakery customers were too busy sampling the goodies, looking straight past her work.

She rearranged the paintings one more time, hoping the new layout would catch someone's eye. Then the bell on the door jingled and Blake and his mother walked in. Her heart kicked up, nervous that they'd be surveying her work, but also thrilled to see him again. And it had only been four hours since she left his apartment.

Or maybe it was the passion bread kicking in.

"Nicole, how are sales? These are beautiful," his mother cooed, immediately drawn to one she'd painted in the park.

"It's been going okay," she lied.

Blake stood, examining at her work. "Would a few of these would add a little personality to my apartment?"

She laughed. "A few paint samples would add a little personality to your apartment."

He tried to look angry, but she saw the corners of his mouth twitch. He strolled through the bakery checking out the paintings. She was as self-conscious as if they were nude pictures of herself hung on the wall.

His mother picked out two of the framed paintings, and Blake hovered in front of the series she did at the cabin. He turned to her. "I want all of these you did up in the mountains."

Mentally doing the math, she silently squealed over the sales. But then she realized as his supposed girlfriend, she would be expected to give them to him. Truth was, she owed him. She could think of it as payment for room and board. "Oh, honey, you can just take them if you want them." She twisted her hands behind her back.

Shaking her head, his mother put her hand on her hip. "Nicole, real artists don't give their work away, not even to loved ones. We'll pay for these like your regular customers. And I simply must talk to my friend about setting up a show at her gallery. Oh, and the prince's ball! He lives in Blake's building and I've already contacted his assistant to inform him you'll be donating a piece for his charity auction to benefit the hospital. Blake will be taking you, of course." She gripped Goldie's arm and lowered her voice. "You're going to make incredible contacts there."

"Great idea, Mom," Blake said.

The bell jangled on the door again, and she was feeling lucky enough to believe she could score another sale.

When she saw who it was, she froze; it was Gloria Midas. Her sister, Veronica, worked at the bakery. Gloria apparently liked to hang around looking for freebie cupcakes. Gloria Midas certainly wouldn't be buying any paintings.

Goldie had the misfortune of meeting her a few days earlier while scouting out the location for setting up her work. And Gloria had noticed the apartment sitter flyers she'd hung up as well. "I'm never going to work," Gloria had said, inspecting the flyer. "Unless you call finding a husband work." Then she cackled.

Now, Gloria clicked across the floor in her high heels and cocked her head, looking at Goldie's paintings. "You've still got a lot of stock here. If you don't sell anything, are you going to have to start working here?"

Blake's mother chuckled. "My dear, Nicole is a lawyer *and* an artist. She doesn't need to work here. Painting is her hobby and she's quite good at it."

Gloria looked stunned, then laughed. "Nicole? You're kidding, right? *Goldie* is an apartment sitter on a good day, and a struggling artist who crashes with her friends on the rest."

His mother's hand hovered over her mouth. "Blake?"

Blake looked ready to defend her. But this was Goldie's chance to make everything right for him. As her heart sunk, she took a deep breath. "I'm sorry Blake, it's true. I've lied to you. I'm not who you think I am." It hurt as much to say it, as if she were truly revealing a lie.

He took a step toward her. "Don't do this…"

She couldn't bear to hear what he'd say. Gathering her purse, she dashed out the door, realizing all her things were still at his place. Didn't matter. She'd stay at Ariel's and arrange to get her things later, then pick up her artwork another day.

She'd left things behind before during her stays: socks, barrettes, and toothbrushes.

But never her heart.

***

Blake paid for his paintings, and his mother's, too. They left the store quickly before that horrible woman could make any more accusations.

"What was that all about?" his mother asked. "That woman was lying about Nicole, right? Right?" She sounded desperate.

He looked up at the sky. This was exactly what he wanted. He could pretend to be devastated by this news, and keep his mother off his back for a while. But in all honesty, he *was* devastated. He liked Goldie. A lot. And he was interested in seeing where this could go with her.

His mother stopped walking and grabbed his arm. "Blake, what's going on?"

"Mom, come back to my place and I'll explain everything."

***

His mother sat in stunned silence as he explained how Goldie came to be his "girlfriend."

She rubbed her temples with the tips of her fingers. "I'm sorry. I didn't realize I was putting so much pressure on you." She sighed. "The thing is, I really like Nicole—I mean, Goldie—even if she isn't a lawyer. And I like what she's done for you. You're happier and more relaxed."

He nodded. "I know. Everything has changed since she showed up."

"Go get her, Blake. Don't let her go."

The thing was, he didn't know where to find her.

Fortunately, she called to get her things the next day. "Goldie, we need to talk."

"About what? I'm sure that got your mother off your back in a real hurry."

"Come over. Let's talk. I want you to see how your paintings look hanging in my apartment."

"That's really kind of you, but let's just cut our losses and move on."

"I'm not ready to move on."

"What are you talking about?"

"I'm not sure. I just know the thought of you leaving my life hurts. And Miss Sniggles will miss you like crazy."

She was quiet for a long moment and he felt hopeful. Then she said, "Blake, it'll never work. I'm not from your world—unless I'm crashing in it, or babysitting a dog. Your toaster probably costs more than everything I own. I'm sorry. I've got to get my life together. Goodbye, Blake. And thank you for everything. I'll be over tomorrow to get my suitcases."

***

Being back at Ariel's was only a temporary situation. With the earnings from her art sale and a job—location yet to be determined—she should be able to get her own place in three months.

She dreaded seeing Blake, but she would be as quick as possible, like she was pulling off a Band-Aid.

Hopefully, the same theory applied for pulling someone out of your heart.

Turned out, it wasn't a problem; he wasn't there when she showed up. His mother answered the door. "Oh, hello. Blake just dashed out."

Goldie's heart sank, not only because secretly she had wanted to see him, but because she couldn't bear to see the disappointment in his mother's eyes, hear the disapproval in her voice.

"I'm just going to quickly gather my things." She headed for the bedroom, but Mrs. Behr stopped her.

"Not so fast," she said.

Here it comes. Well, she deserved it. She raised her head to face her.

There was concern in Mrs. Behr's eyes. "Why are you doing this? I know you and Blake care deeply about each other. Anyone could see that."

Goldie steeled herself. "But it was just a charade. I'm not who you thought I was."

"You weren't deceiving Blake. You were helping him deceive me, and I can get over that. I was hard on him."

Miss Sniggles came tearing out of her room and pranced around Goldie's feet, which certainly didn't help. She reached down and scratched the dog's ear, unwilling to pick her up. "He's a lawyer. I'm practically homeless. He needs a different kind of girl."

His mother shook his head. "You're creative and brave. You followed your dreams when no one else believed in you. Me? I gave up my art the first time someone disapproved. Blake abandoned his love of writing when I expressed my concern. But you have passion and commitment. Blake is different because of you. He's a better person; he's truer to himself. This apartment, all these things he has are nice. But they don't make him happy." She pointed at her. "You do."

Goldie shook her head, and caught her thumbs in the belt loops on her jeans. "I have to get my act together before I could try a relationship with him. I've been living a vagabond life. It's embarrassing, looking back now. I can't just move in with him and pick up where we left off. He'd always wonder if I was just with him because it was convenient."

His mother sighed. "So you have something to prove. I can understand that."

Goldie made her way to the bedroom, with the dog on her heels. Tears welled in her eyes when she saw her paintings hung in the hall; they looked perfect, like they belonged there. Too bad she didn't.

She jammed her things in her suitcases, picked up his robe and smelled him one more time, then left the room.

His mother was waiting at the door for her. She handed her a business card. "Stop by this boutique. I bought a dress for you that will be perfect for the prince's ball. But of course, if you don't like it, you can choose something else."

Goldie stared at the card. "I don't understand. Why would I be going to the ball with Blake now?"

"You're not. You're going as the artist who donated a beautiful painting for the charity auction. And all my friends are going to be there, and they're simply dying to talk to you about commissions for their home. I'd be terribly embarrassed if I had to tell them you weren't coming now."

She shook her head. "You're just being kind. I'm not so sure I can make a living from my art. You and Blake were just being nice buying my stuff."

Mrs. Behr put her hand on her hip. "Goldie, after you left, someone came and bought all your work."

"One person? Who?"

"The owner's grandmother, Kate Robinson. She loved your work. She'll be at the ball, too, and wants to meet you. And of course, her granddaughter, Rose, will be there with her boyfriend. He's my personal trainer, you know. Come on. It'll be fun!"

Goldie frowned. "Will Blake be there?"

His mother shook her head. "I'm not sure. But you'll come, right?"

"You've been so wonderful to me. Of course I will."

***

Mrs. Behr had picked out a beautiful strapless dress of midnight blue for Goldie. As she turned to inspect herself in the mirror, she realized she'd never worn anything so stunning. The cost of the dress would probably cover rent for a month at a small studio apartment, but she was determined to enjoy herself and be a professional. She couldn't pass up this opportunity to make some new clients and sock away some money.

Later that night, on the elevator ride up to the penthouse of Grimm Towers, her fingers shook as she gripped her clutch, loaded with business cards she'd just had made. When the elevator zoomed past the seventh floor, she thought of Blake and sighed.

She spotted a uniformed butler standing outside a door and presumed it was the prince's place. He welcomed her and opened the door for her. She was hit by sudden wave of nerves. All these important people; all these rich people. Would they know she was a fraud?

She scanned the ornate ballroom, bigger than she could've imagined would be in an apartment. Classical music played, waiters circulated with champagne and hors d'oeuvres. An elaborate display was filled with whimsical cupcakes and desserts. Goldie spotted Rose from the bakery and rushed over, pleased to see someone she knew.

"How did you land this gig?"

Rose grinned. "The prince loves our Sea Goddess muffins." She frowned. "Although he didn't order any for the party." She shrugged. "Hey, I've got loads of money for you from you art sale. Stop by Monday and I'll pay you." She pulled a handsome man toward her. "Let me introduce my boyfriend, Jack Wolff."

She shook hands with a gorgeous, buff man and wondered how much passion bread she'd plied him with; he looked utterly smitten with her.

Then three women in aprons hurried over. Rose sighed. "Ladies, I need you to man the table so I can circulate and talk with the guests."

Goldie willed her jaw not to drop. Veronica and Gloria scurried behind the table, aprons tied on over their elegant dresses. "Hello, Gloria. I didn't know you'd be here. *Working,*" Goldie added. "Have you taken on a part-time job?"

Gloria stuck her nose in the air. "My mother, sister, and I are volunteering."

Goldie nodded, "Oh, I see."

"Of course, we didn't realize that until we got here," their mother said through her teeth.

Veronica dusted her hands. "I said I could get you into the ball, I guess I forgot to mention that small detail." She winked at Goldie.

Veronica's mother hissed at her. "Take off your apron. Here comes Jeremy James. You can't give up on him yet."

Veronica rolled her eyes. "Mother, when the right guy comes along, I'll know. And Jeremy is not the right guy for me."

"And just what are you going to do until then?" her mother asked.

"Work at the bakery. Go to cooking school." She shrugged as Jeremy and his girlfriend approached.

Goldie did a double take. "Shawna White? From Central High? Is that you?"

Shawna squealed and hugged Goldie. "You look great. I heard you were in the city working as an artist. I ran into your mother at the grocery store last time I was home. She's so proud of you chasing your dreams in the city." Then she twisted her lips, uncertain. "But she wants you to get your cello out of her house."

Goldie laughed. "Thanks for the tip. How are you?"

Shawna held out her left hand and wiggled her fingers, showing off a beautiful engagement ring. "I'm about to become a wife and stepmother to seven kids."

Veronica came from behind the table and reached for Shawna's hand. "I just have to say congratulations. I'm sorry for any trouble I caused you two." Then she dropped her voice to a whisper. "And I do hope you're a better stepmother than I was to you." She plucked a muffin off the table and offered it to Shawna. "Apple strudel muffin? I made it myself."

She held up her hand and took a step back. "No thanks, I think we're good." And with that, they headed across the ballroom.

"Cupcake or a muffin?" Veronica offered Goldie. "Are you feeling naughty or nice?"

More like nervous, she thought. *Is there a dessert for that?* A pumpkin muffin certainly wouldn't help. "A cupcake, definitely a cupcake." She took a beautiful treat and wandered over to the auction table. Certificates for weekend stays in Europe and the Caribbean were being auctioned off, with the silent bidding already in the thousands. Jewelry and Jiminy Shoes were available for bids. And next to a crystal vase sat her painting of kids playing along the shore at the cottage. She bit her lip before getting the courage to look at the bids written down. When she glanced at the paper, she gasped. Six hundred dollars?

"I'm surprised it isn't higher."

She spun around, shocked to see Blake standing there, smiling. "I didn't think you were coming," she said.

"I suspect my mother told you that just to make sure you came."

She pursed her lips. "Blake, it's not that I don't like you, it's just that I don't like where I'm at right now. You know?"

He stepped closer to her. She could smell his aftershave and tried not to inhale. "I know," he said.

"You made me realize I feel the same way about myself. Which is why I quit my job."

She covered her mouth. "What?"

"You were willing to be homeless to pursue your passion. I gave up my passion just to have nice things. I figure there's got to be a middle ground for the two of us."

She hugged her arms around herself, not wanting to believe what he was saying. "What are you going to do?"

He grinned, looking entirely pleased with himself. "I'm opening my own law firm specializing in contract negotiation for writers and artists. It'll be a much easier schedule that'll leave me time to write."

She couldn't help it; she launched herself into his arms. "I'm so happy for you."

He held her tight. "Me too. I'm excited. And I'm so grateful to you for inspiring me." His smile disappeared. "But I can't afford my place anymore. I'm going to be moving out."

She reached for his hand and squeezed it. "That's too bad. I know you love it."

"Doesn't matter. I'll find a new place. And I sure could use a roommate to help pay the rent."

Her heart dropped. Roommate? Did he only think of her as a friend? She let her hand slide out of his.

But he grabbed it back with a grin. "Especially if that roommate is someone I'm falling in love with." Then he tipped up her chin and kissed her. "Shall we go apartment shopping tomorrow?"

"You'll let me keep my cello, there, right?"

He laughed. "Absolutely. Now come on, I want you to meet a few people who will be crazy for your art."

Blake introduced her to the prince who was throwing the ball to benefit the hospital that saved his future father-in-law's life, and performed plastic surgeries on the prince's scars. "I'll have to commission you to paint a picture of my future wife, Belle. I'd love to unveil it at the wedding."

Belle rolled her eyes. "Only if she does one of you."
His hand went to his face, fingering his scar.

"I don't have to include the scar," Goldie said, softly.
It was noticeable, but not horrible.

He shook his head. "No, you do. It's part of who I
am now. I'm not ashamed."

"And I could build gorgeous frames for them," Belle
said, the gears her mind obviously whirling.

"You do framing? Custom frames would be
incredible." Goldie fished out a business card and
handed it to her. "Let's talk this week."

Belle took the card with a smile. "I'll call you. Now
if you'll excuse me, I need to find my father."

The prince shook his head. "Leave him be. He's
talking with my neighbor, Kate Robinson. I have the
feeling they don't want to be interrupted."

Goldie looked over at the older man and woman
nearly head to head sharing a joke. "It was so nice to
meet you both," Goldie said, leaving them to their other
guests.

"See?" Blake said as they headed for the balcony.
"You're going to have more work than you know what to
do with."

As they headed outside, they realized a couple was
already out there, kissing. It was the butler who'd let her
in and a woman in a maid's outfit. They quickly broke
their kiss. "Yes, that will be all for now Mrs. Downing,"
the man said, clearing his throat.

"Of course, Reginald," she said, smoothing her hair
back in place.

Goldie quickly ducked back inside to give them their
privacy—and promptly bumped into another couple.

"I'm sorry," Goldie said. Then she froze. "Hey,
you're the girl with the crystal shoes! I met you at a bar
during that crazy week of yours!"

"Yes, I'm Cindi."

Goldie looked at the woman's feet. "I thought you
had to give them up. How'd you get them back?"

Cindi grinned. "An early wedding gift from the Jiminy Shoes owner."

Goldie whistled, imagining exactly how she'd paint them if given the chance.

Rose's grandmother, Kate, approached them. "Goldie! Just the person I was looking for."

"Mrs. Robinson. I can't thank you enough for buying my work. I don't know what to say."

"You're very talented. After seeing your work at my granddaughter's bakery, I'd like to hire you for a new ad campaign for Jiminy Shoes. Think you can paint Cindi in those crystal shoes? We're launching a new line of affordable versions and I want something special to kick off the campaign."

"You work for Jiminy Shoes?" Goldie asked.

Mrs. Robinson winked. "You could say I got my foot in the door when it first started."

Goldie handed her a card with promises to talk later in the week.

Blake led her across the ballroom and snatched two glasses of champagne for them. "To our new start," he proposed, holding up his glass.

"To our new apartment," Goldie said, clinking his glass. "We're going to have to find a place with a studio for me now that I've got all this work lined up."

"Nothing too big," he said. "We won't be able to afford it yet."

"But nothing too small. Miss Sniggles has her standards, you know."

He leaned toward her and stole a kiss. "I know we'll find something just right."

"How do you know?"

"Everything's been right since you broke into my apartment."

She tried to protest, but he stole her words with a kiss that promised a happy ending no matter where they landed.

They were interrupted by the ringing of a bell. "Ladies and gentlemen," announced the butler. "Please line up in the hallway. We are promptly commencing with rides down the banister."

About the Author

Lisa Scott is a former TV news anchor who know enjoys making up stories for a living. She's also a voice actor living in upstate New York with her kids, hubby, cats, dog, and koi fish. Check out her website at ReadLisaScott.com, and sign up for her newsletter to be notified about new releases. Like her on Facebook at Read Lisa Scott.

CPSIA information can be obtained
at www.ICGtesting.com
Printed in the USA
LVHW102235311022
732057LV00022B/237

9 781481 289993